Harley Heartbeats:

The Forbidden Ride

By
Wild Billy Mitchell

Published by Kinetic Digital Publishers

www.kineticdigitalpublishers.com

For permissions, inquiries, or other correspondence, please visit our website.

TABLE OF CONTENTS

Chapter 1

The Open Road Beckons

The roar of a Harley Davidson engine, a symphony of power and freedom, always promised more than just a ride; it whispered of escape, of unbound possibilities. For Jake 'Maverick' Riley, that promise had become a deliberate strategy, a calculated risk to inject a much-needed jolt of adrenaline into the comfortable, yet increasingly predictable, rhythm of his marriage to Sarah. He envisioned the open road as the ultimate aphrodisiac, a potent elixir to rekindle a passion that had, perhaps, settled into too gentle a simmer. This weekend, with two close friends joining them, was meticulously planned not just as a trip, but as an adventure designed to push boundaries and rediscover the exhilarating edges of their shared desire.

Jake, with his charismatic grin and an entrepreneurial spirit that thrived on risk, believed in the transformative power of experience. His well-built frame, though softened slightly by a 'beer belly' he carried with confident good humor, belied a sharp mind constantly seeking the next thrill. He'd orchestrated this motorcycle adventure, the 'Forbidden Ride,' with a singular, fervent hope: to reawaken the wild spark that had first drawn him to Sarah. Every twist of the throttle, every mile devoured by their Harleys, was intended as a step closer to a profound, exhilarating reconnection, a return to the raw, untamed essence of their bond.

Sarah 'Vixen' Riley, Jake's stunning wife, possessed a captivating allure that turned heads effortlessly, a fact she was acutely, if sometimes uncomfortably, aware of. Her beautiful set of breasts and a great ass, combined with the vibrant energy of a hot young woman and the astute wisdom of a middle-aged wife, made her a potent presence. Initially, a flicker of hesitation had crossed her mind regarding the trip's intensity, a subtle unease about the unspoken expectations Jake might harbor. Yet, beneath that apprehension stirred her own longing for excitement, a yearning to feel desired and to embrace the bolder facets of her sensuality, an adventurous attitude that often manifested as 'Let's Roll' with very little clothing.

The initial plan for the Harley road trip had involved a couple of friends and their wives, a convivial gathering of familiar faces. However, the capricious hand of fate intervened, leaving one wife ill and the other friend, David, currently unmarried. This unexpected turn of events presented a singular and intriguing dynamic: two riding buddies, including myself, embarking on this journey with my wife, Sarah, as the sole female companion. The very notion of this altered adventure, the close quarters and heightened intimacy it promised, stirred a primal rumble deep within my groin, a potent foreshadowing of the excitements to come.

Adding to this already charged atmosphere was Mark 'Rebel' Johnson, a long-time friend of Jake's, whose brooding intensity and quiet charm belied a simmering secret. Tall, slim, and notably well-endowed, Mark had always been a ladies' man, though his most significant, unexpressed desire remained fixed on Sarah. His presence on this trip was a profound test of his loyalty to Jake and his own self-control, each mile a silent battle against years of suppressed longing. A faint, almost imperceptible smile would often grace his lips whenever Sarah was near, a silent testament to the depth of his forbidden admiration.

Then there was David 'Rider' Chen, the newest addition to their inner circle, an easy-going, flirtatious soul whose pragmatic approach to pleasure often served as a playful catalyst. Of average build yet surprisingly strong and agile, David was married to Lisa, who, unfortunately, couldn't make the trip, a circumstance he often lamented due to their recent marital problems. His candid complaints about Lisa's months-long sexual 'cut-off' hinted at a profound, almost desperate horniness, a frustration that made him acutely attuned to the sensual undercurrents of their group, ready to climb a wall, or perhaps, explore new avenues of release.

As the engines collectively roared to life, a palpable wave of anticipation washed over the quartet, a shared breath of exhilarating freedom. The bikes, gleaming chrome and throbbing power, were not just machines, but extensions of their collective desire to escape the mundane, to shed the constraints of everyday life. The promise of the open road, stretching endlessly before them, was a siren song, beckoning them towards uncharted territories, both literal and metaphorical. Each rider felt the potent pull of adventure, a thrilling sense of liberation that promised more than just scenic vistas; it hinted at profound, personal revelations.

The journey ahead, particularly the whispered legend of the 'Forbidden Trail,' loomed as more than just a challenging detour; it represented a literal and symbolic descent into uncharted emotional terrain. This was where the dangerous dance of temptation would truly begin, where the lines between friendship and desire, loyalty and longing, would blur under the intoxicating influence of freedom and close proximity. The unique dynamic of three men and one very attractive wife, hurtling down highways and hidden paths, was a crucible designed to test the very foundations of their relationships, pushing each character to confront their deepest, most unspoken desires.

This was not merely a motorcycle trip; it was a pilgrimage into the heart of desire, a bold exploration of what it truly meant to rediscover passion and intimacy when faced with the thrill of the forbidden. Loyalties would be challenged, personal boundaries would be tested, and the very definition of their relationships stood poised for redefinition. As they rode towards 'The Oasis' Motel, the ultimate destination of this audacious adventure, the promise of the ride transformed into an electrifying question, hanging heavy in the air: could they navigate the intoxicating allure of forbidden attraction and emerge, not just intact, but profoundly transformed?

Jake 'Maverick' Riley saw his marriage with Sarah not as a problem, but as an opportunity, a thrilling venture ripe for reinvestment. He believed the open road, the roar of a Harley beneath them, held the potent magic to strip away the mundane and reignite the smoldering embers of their shared passion. This weekend wasn't just a trip; it was a meticulously orchestrated journey designed to inject a much-needed jolt of excitement back into their lives, a testament to his unwavering confidence and his penchant for orchestrating grand, exhilarating experiences. His heart pounded with a familiar anticipation, the kind that always accompanied his biggest gambles, both in business and in love. He envisioned Sarah, his stunning 'Vixen,' embracing the intoxicating freedom, her inhibitions melting away with every mile. This was his vision, bold and unyielding, a promise of rediscovery.

His entrepreneurial spirit, accustomed to pushing boundaries and taking calculated risks, now focused entirely on their relationship. Jake had always found the ultimate aphrodisiac in the thrill of the chase, the unknown winding path, and he was convinced this adventure would remind Sarah of the wild, passionate woman he'd fallen in love with. He yearned for her to shed the last vestiges of everyday life, to let her stunning beauty and untamed spirit blaze forth, uninhibited by routine. He wanted to see that adventurous spark in her eyes again, the one that once mirrored his own audacious soul. The very thought of her, unbound and exhilarated, sent a familiar rumble deep in his groin, a prelude to the excitement he craved.

He imagined Sarah's initial hesitation transforming into an eager embrace of the journey, her beautiful breasts rising and falling with excited breaths, her great ass swaying with the bike's rhythm. Jake knew his wife; beneath her intelligent and observant demeanor lay a profound sensuality, a 'hot middle-aged wife' ready to shed any lingering self-consciousness. He pictured her infectious smile, a beacon of joy, as she surrendered to the intoxicating freedom of the road, her adventurous attitude truly taking hold. This trip was designed to awaken that core part of her, to remind them both of the raw, undeniable attraction that had always pulsed between them, a fire he was determined to stoke.

Mark 'Rebel' Johnson and David 'Rider' Chen, their close friends and riding companions, were vital pieces of this intricate puzzle. Jake valued their camaraderie, but he also recognized the subtle, unspoken tension their presence might add, a competitive undercurrent he subconsciously welcomed. Mark, with his brooding intensity and quiet admiration for Sarah, and David, with his easy flirtation and frustrations with his own marriage, would undoubtedly heighten the charged atmosphere. Jake, ever the orchestrator, saw their various dynamics as fuel for the fire he intended to ignite, a thrilling challenge to his own claim on Sarah's attention and affection.

The 'Forbidden Trail' was more than just an off-road path; it represented the heart of Jake's vision, a literal and metaphorical journey into uncharted territory. He relished the idea of pushing past the familiar, delving into secluded spots where the rules of the everyday world dissolved, where desires could surface, unbidden and unjudged. This less-traveled route, known only to a select few, symbolized the adventurous leap they were taking, a deliberate step into the thrilling unknown. He believed this shared experience of venturing beyond conventional boundaries would irrevocably deepen their bond, forging a new, more intense connection.

Beyond the immediate thrill and the physical excitement, Jake harbored a deeper longing to reconnect with Sarah on a profound emotional level. He understood that true intimacy wasn't just about the rush of adrenaline or the heat of passion, but about shared vulnerability and renewed understanding. This trip, with its escalating forbidden desires, was his way of tearing down any walls that had subtly risen between them, forcing them to confront their deepest needs. He wanted to prove to Sarah, and perhaps to himself, that their relationship possessed a depth capable of encompassing both wild adventure and genuine emotional closeness, a balance he was still learning to master.

The 'Oasis' Motel, a nondescript beacon on the horizon, loomed large in his mind not merely as a rest stop, but as the crucible where their renewed passion would be forged. Jake envisioned the culmination of the trip's escalating tensions within its private walls, a space where unspoken desires would finally be confronted and perhaps acted upon. This was where loyalties would be tested, where the true meaning of intimacy would be redefined, and where the 'one motel room adventure' would unfold. He anticipated a night of raw honesty and uninhibited exploration, a testament to the courage they both possessed to embrace their desires.

Jake's determination was unwavering; he would make this trip a monumental success for their marriage, transforming routine into a vibrant, unforgettable journey. His confident masculinity, tempered by a playful innuendo, masked a genuine desire to see Sarah truly thrive, to rediscover the passion that had always defined them. He knew the risks were high, the temptations potent, but Jake Riley had always thrived on the edge. This weekend was not just about rekindling a flame; it was about forging an entirely new, hotter fire, one that would burn brighter and bolder than ever before, cementing their bond in the thrilling crucible of the forbidden road.

The low rumble of Jake's Harley, a familiar heartbeat against the asphalt, promised an adventure Sarah 'Vixen' Riley both craved and subtly dreaded. She watched him, his frame still powerful despite the slight beer belly, radiating an almost boyish enthusiasm for the open road and the 'spark' he so desperately sought to reignite. His vision of this trip, a high-octane aphrodisiac for their marriage, resonated deep within her, stirring a complex cocktail of longing and a faint, almost imperceptible tremor of apprehension. Sarah knew Jake, understood his penchant for risk, and recognized that this weekend was less about scenic routes and more about uncharted emotional terrain, a journey into the very heart of their shared, yet sometimes routine, passion. The thought alone sent a shiver down her spine, a silent acknowledgment of the exhilarating, perhaps dangerous, path ahead.

Her hesitation wasn't rooted in fear of the unknown, but rather in a sharp, intelligent awareness of the unspoken desires lurking beneath the surface of Jake's grand plan. Sarah, observant and intuitive, saw beyond the chrome and leather, recognizing the subtle glint in her husband's eyes a hunger not just for her, but for the thrill of pushing boundaries, for the delicious tension of shared transgression. She had always been the emotional anchor, the one who navigated the intricate currents of their relationship, yet this time, Jake was steering them into waters she suspected might be far rougher, far more exhilarating, than he openly admitted. Her mind, ever analytical, processed the implications, weighing the potential for rekindled passion against the precarious balance of their existing world.

Yet, beneath that careful calculation, a potent anticipation simmered, an almost primal yearning for the validation and unbridled desire she sometimes felt was slipping through their grasp. Sarah, with her stunning beauty and captivating allure, was accustomed to being admired, but she yearned for more than just surface appreciation; she longed for a deeper, more visceral connection, a rediscovery of the 'Vixen' within. The promise of this trip, of shedding the mundane and embracing the raw freedom of the road, offered an intoxicating escape, a chance to reclaim not just Jake's attention, but her own potent sensuality. She was, after all, a woman who often wore very little, her adventurous spirit encapsulated in her mantra: 'Let's Roll'.

Her reflection in the mirror, even in the muted light of their bedroom, confirmed the undeniable truth: she possessed the body of a hot young woman, perfectly complemented by a beautiful set of breasts and a great ass, all imbued with the knowledge and confidence of a hot middle-aged wife. This wasn't vanity; it was an acknowledgment of her power, a tool she was ready to wield in the service of their marriage, or perhaps, in the service of her own awakening desires. She knew the effect she had on men —a silent hum of appreciation that followed her. On this trip, with Jake's unspoken agenda, that effect would be amplified, becoming an integral part of their journey into the forbidden.

The presence of Mark 'Rebel' Johnson and David 'Rider' Chen added another layer to her burgeoning anticipation, a subtle thrum of electricity she couldn't ignore. Mark, with his brooding intensity and the long-held, unspoken desire she sensed simmering beneath his stoic exterior, and David, with his easy flirtatiousness and pragmatic appreciation for beauty, were not merely companions. They were catalysts, their gazes, their casual remarks, their very presence, serving to heighten the charged atmosphere. Sarah was acutely aware of the competitive undercurrent that flowed between the men, especially concerning her, and a part of her, the 'Vixen' Jake sought to reawaken, found a thrilling, almost dangerous, excitement in it.

This journey, particularly the infamous 'Forbidden Trail' David had hinted at, felt like a literal and metaphorical descent into uncharted territory, a path designed to strip away inhibitions and expose raw desires. Sarah understood the symbolism, the deliberate choice to venture beyond the familiar, and a thrilling sense of readiness began to eclipse her initial reservations. She was prepared to push boundaries, to navigate the complex interplay of loyalty and longing, and to confront the unspoken attractions that would inevitably surface in such close quarters. The road, she knew, would offer more than just scenic views; it would offer revelations.

The trip was less a vacation and more a crucible, designed to test the very foundations of their marriage and her own sense of self. Sarah wasn't just a passenger; she was an active participant in this daring experiment, ready to explore the limits of her own desires and the strength of her commitment. She understood Jake's need for excitement, his entrepreneurial spirit of risk-taking now applied to their intimate life, and she was willing to meet him there, to rediscover the passion that had first bound them together. This wasn't merely about reigniting a flame; it was about forging a new, perhaps hotter, one.

As the final preparations were made, a confident smile, both mischievous and resolute, touched Sarah's lips. The hum of the Harleys was no longer a vague promise but a direct summons, pulling her towards an adventure that promised to redefine intimacy and challenge every expectation. She was ready for the open road, ready for the close quarters, and undeniably, ready for whatever forbidden desires might surface when three men and one very attractive wife embarked upon their ultimate ride. The anticipation was a living thing, a thrilling pulse beneath her skin, propelling her towards the unknown.

The 'Midnight Run' bar throbbed with a raw, electric pulse, a symphony of classic rock and the low hum of anticipation. Outside, a squadron of Harleys gleamed under the sparse streetlights, their chrome catching the neon glow of the bar's skull-and-crossbones sign. Jake 'Maverick' Riley pulled Sarah 'Vixen' Riley closer, relishing the feel of her curves against his side, the scent of leather and her subtle perfume mingling in the smoky air. This was their starting line, a place where inhibitions shed like worn-out tires, and the open road called with a siren song of freedom.

Jake's grin was wide, almost predatory, as he surveyed the dimly lit interior. He'd orchestrated this trip, this carefully planned descent into the thrilling unknown, specifically to reignite the spark that sometimes flickered under the weight of routine. Watching Sarah, radiant and undeniably alluring in her fitted leather, he felt a familiar rumble deep in his gut, a mix of possessiveness and a hungry excitement for what the weekend promised. Tonight was about setting the stage, about letting the subtle currents of desire begin their dance.

Sarah, ever the captivating 'Vixen,' moved with an innate grace that drew every eye in the room, her smile a beacon of playful invitation. Her beautiful breasts were subtly accentuated by her leather vest, and her ass, a masterpiece of curves, was impossible to ignore as she navigated the crowded space. She knew the attention she commanded, felt the appreciative glances, and rather than shrinking from them, she met them with a confident, almost mischievous glint in her eyes. This trip, she realized, was as much about her own awakening as it was about Jake's grand plan.

Mark 'Rebel' Johnson was already at their usual corner booth, a brooding silhouette against the flickering neon. His gaze, however, wasn't on the flickering lights, but instantly found Sarah. A subtle tightening around his jaw was the only tell of the battle raging beneath his stoic exterior, a conflict between his long-held, unspoken desire for Jake's wife and his unwavering loyalty to his friend. He offered a tight, almost forced smile, his tall, lean frame exuding a quiet intensity that was both intriguing and a little dangerous.

Moments later, David 'Rider' Chen sauntered in, his easy charm a stark contrast to Mark's intensity. "Maverick, Vixen!" he called out, his voice a playful drawl, his eyes lingering on Sarah a beat too long. "Ready to escape the chains of domesticity?" He winked, a clear nod to his own marital frustrations, a sly hint at the sexual drought he often complained about. David, ever the instigator, seemed to thrive on the charged atmosphere, his presence adding another layer of unpredictable energy to their small group.

With the four of them finally gathered, a palpable tension settled into the booth, a silent hum beneath the bar's raucous music. Jake caught Mark's lingering glance at Sarah, then David's more overt appreciation, and a thrill, both possessive and provocative, shot through him. He loved the idea of his wife being desired, a testament to her allure, even as it tested the boundaries of their shared adventure. Sarah, in turn, felt the weight of their gazes, a delicious warmth spreading through her, a silent acknowledgment of the forbidden dance about to begin.

"So, the 'Forbidden Trail' tomorrow, huh?" David leaned forward, his voice low, a conspiratorial glint in his eye. "Heard it's a real challenge, a place where the road bites back if you're not careful." Jake nodded, his own excitement building. "That's the point, Rider. We're not looking for a scenic drive; we're looking for an adventure that pushes us, that wakes us up." He squeezed Sarah's knee under the table, a silent promise of the exhilaration to come, both on the asphalt and beyond.

Sarah's heart quickened at the mention of the 'Forbidden Trail.' It sounded dangerous, thrilling, a direct challenge to her cautious nature. Yet, looking at the eager faces of the men, and feeling Jake's possessive touch, a different kind of excitement began to bubble within her. It was the thrill of the unknown, the allure of stepping outside her comfort zone, a chance to rediscover a wilder, more uninhibited part of herself. She met Jake's gaze, a silent agreement passing between them, an unspoken pact to embrace whatever the trail, and the trip, had in store.

As the night deepened, the clinking of glasses and the roar of the band became a backdrop to their escalating anticipation. The 'Midnight Run' was more than just a bar; it was a crucible where their journey truly began, a place where the boundaries of friendship and desire blurred. The air crackled with unspoken desires and the thrilling promise of a weekend designed to push every limit. Tomorrow, the Harleys would roar, and the forbidden ride would truly begin, leading them down a path from which none of them might return unchanged.

Mark 'Rebel' Johnson leaned against his customized Harley, the low thrum of its engine a familiar comfort, yet his usual stoic demeanor was laced with an unfamiliar tension. His gaze, often distant and assessing, now kept an almost furtive track of Sarah, her laughter a bright, intoxicating melody amidst the bar's raucous din. Years of suppressed longing for Jake's vibrant wife, a secret held tightly within the confines of their shared brotherhood, felt precariously close to fracturing under the weight of this audacious road trip. The very thought of the upcoming 'Forbidden Trail' ignited a dangerous spark in his gut, warring fiercely with his deep-seated loyalty to his friend, Jake. He had always prided himself on his discipline, a trait honed during his military days, but Sarah's undeniable allure threatened to unravel every carefully constructed barrier.

Across the dimly lit space, David 'Rider' Chen, the newest addition to their tight-knit circle, effortlessly exuded an easygoing charm, his eyes twinkling with an almost impish delight. Unlike Mark's brooding intensity, David's appreciation for Sarah was openly expressed, a playful glint in his gaze that held no pretense of hidden agendas, only genuine admiration. His own marital frustrations with Lisa, a dull ache of sexual neglect that had festered for months, fueled a pragmatic hedonism, a willingness to embrace the thrill of the moment without the heavy emotional baggage. For David, this trip was an escape, an opportunity to revel in the camaraderie and the sheer uninhibited freedom of the open road, perhaps even to find a fleeting spark of excitement that had long been absent from his own bed.

The contrast between the two men was stark, yet strangely complementary, like two opposing forces drawn into the same orbit by the magnetic pull of the journey and, more acutely, by Sarah's captivating presence. Mark wrestled with an internal storm of devotion and desire, his every interaction with Sarah a delicate dance between friendship and forbidden yearning. David, conversely, floated through the charged atmosphere with an almost detached amusement, a shrewd observer and occasional instigator, his lighthearted banter often cutting through the unspoken tension like a sharp blade, yet always landing with a disarming smile. Their individual approaches to desire, one deeply internal and agonizing, the other external and almost flippant, set a complex rhythm for the adventure ahead.

Despite their differing internal landscapes, a shared history on the asphalt bound them, a camaraderie forged through countless miles and the unspoken understanding of fellow riders. Jake had always been the anchor, the charismatic leader who brought them together, and their loyalty to him, though now tested, was a foundational element of their friendship. They understood the language of roaring engines, the exhilaration of leaning into a sharp curve, and the profound sense of liberation that only the open road could provide. This shared passion transcended their individual complexities, creating a superficial unity that, for the moment, held the simmering undercurrents of desire in check, allowing the illusion of a simple friends' trip to persist.

Sarah's radiant presence, her confident stride, and the way her eyes seemed to hold a world of unspoken secrets, amplified the unspoken desires circulating among the men. For Mark, every casual touch, every shared glance, was a potent reminder of the life he secretly yearned for, a life that belonged to Jake. He found himself constantly battling the urge to protect her, to claim her, even as his conscience screamed betrayal, creating a palpable internal conflict that radiated from his tightly controlled posture. The knowledge that he was riding alongside his best friend, harboring such intense, illicit thoughts about his wife, was a torment he could barely endure, yet one he couldn't bring himself to abandon.

David, ever the pragmatist, subtly fueled the burgeoning tension, his playful provocations and knowing glances encouraging the group to shed their inhibitions. He found a certain thrill in observing the intricate dance of attraction, especially between Mark and Sarah, even as he openly appreciated Sarah's curves and quick wit. His frank discussions about his own marital woes and his longing for sexual excitement, though seemingly self-deprecating, served as an unspoken permission slip for others to acknowledge their own desires. He was a catalyst, a mirror reflecting the uninhibited spirit of the road, challenging the conventional boundaries without ever explicitly breaching them, thereby making the forbidden feel a little less intimidating, a little more attainable.

As the Harleys devoured the miles, leaving the city's neon glow behind, the unspoken desires and burgeoning attractions among the companions solidified into a palpable force. The promise of the 'Forbidden Trail,' whispered about with a mix of trepidation and anticipation, loomed large, a symbol of the untamed desires they were about to confront. And beyond that, the anonymous comfort of 'The Oasis' Motel beckoned, a place where loyalties would undoubtedly be challenged, and the true meaning of intimacy, perhaps even its most forbidden forms, would be redefined. The journey was only just beginning, and the road ahead promised to be as exhilarating as it was dangerous, pulling them all into a dance of temptation that few would emerge from unchanged.

Chapter 2

Cruising into Temptation

The growl of my Harley, 'The Maverick,' vibrated through the worn leather of my vest, a primal symphony harmonizing with the thrumming rock emanating from 'The Midnight Run' bar. Tonight marked the beginning of our escape, a weekend adventure I'd meticulously planned to inject some much-needed adrenaline back into Sarah and my marriage. The air, thick with the scent of exhaust fumes, stale beer, and anticipation, felt like a potent aphrodisiac, promising more than just open roads. My gut tightened with a familiar excitement, a deep rumble that extended beyond the engine, hinting at the thrilling possibilities ahead. This trip wasn't merely about miles; it was about rediscovering the wild pulse that once defined us, pushing boundaries we hadn't dared to approach in years. I watched the last rays of the setting sun glint off the chrome, feeling a surge of confident purpose for the journey about to unfold. This was the moment for us to truly live, to feel every heartbeat.

Sarah, my 'Vixen,' emerged from the bar's shadowed entrance, her silhouette framed by the neon glow, instantly commanding every eye in the lot. Dressed in form-fitting black leather that hugged her incredible curves, she moved with an effortless grace, a vibrant contrast to the rough-and-tumble surroundings. Her smile, a beacon of playful allure, softened the edges of her adventurous spirit, yet her eyes held a spark of knowing mischief. She possessed a body that defied time, a testament to her vibrant energy, and a mind that was sharp, observant, and always ready for life's next thrill. My chest swelled with a potent mix of pride and possessiveness; she was mine, yet I knew her allure was a shared spectacle, a truth that both thrilled and subtly challenged me. Her presence alone promised an electrifying journey, a testament to her captivating power.

Mark 'Rebel' Johnson, lean and intense, leaned against his 'Outlaw,' his gaze following Sarah with an almost imperceptible longing that I, as his long-time friend, had learned to recognize. HHer proximity momentarily softened his usual stoicism, a silent testament to the unspoken history between them, a history he meticulously suppressed. David 'Rider' Chen, ever the charmer, clapped me on the shoulder, his grin wide and infectious, his eyes, however, lingered on Sarah a beat too long. 'Ready for some real road therapy, Maverick?' he quipped, his tone light but his underlying hunger for escape palpable, a hunger born from his own marital frustrations. The dynamic was set: three men, one captivating woman, and the vast, unwritten highway stretching before us.

With a synchronized roar, the three Harleys burst to life, a symphony of power and promise that vibrated through the very ground beneath our boots. The 'Midnight Run' bar, with its lingering whispers of anticipation, quickly receded in our rearview mirrors, swallowed by the encroaching twilight. The cool evening air whipped past our faces, carrying away the last vestiges of city life, replacing them with the heady scent of freedom and the open road. We carved a path onto the main highway, a ribbon of asphalt stretching endlessly into the horizon, each turn a promise of the unknown. The sheer exhilaration of the moment, the raw power beneath us, felt like a cleansing fire, burning away the mundane and igniting a primal sense of adventure. This was the moment we truly began to shed our everyday skins, embracing the untamed spirit of the ride.

The highway unfurled before us like a boundless canvas, each mile painting a new landscape of liberation and possibility. We rode in a loose formation, a silent pact of camaraderie and shared purpose, the rhythmic thrum of our engines a constant, reassuring heartbeat. The city's oppressive weight lifted with every passing mile, giving way to an expansive sense of peace and a profound connection to the raw, unfiltered world. Sunlight, now a golden hue, cast long shadows as we sped through rolling hills and open plains, the wind a constant, exhilarating force against our bodies. This was the essence of why we rode: to chase that elusive feeling of absolute freedom, to taste the unbridled wildness that only the road could offer. It was a journey into the heart of exhilaration, a collective pursuit of pure, unadulterated passion.

Beside me, Sarah, initially a touch reserved, began to visibly transform, shedding her inhibitions with each mile we devoured. Her laughter, carried on the wind, now mingled freely with the engine's roar, a melody of pure, unadulterated joy. She leaned into the curves with increasing confidence, her body a fluid extension of her powerful machine, her spirit blossoming under the vast, open sky. I could feel her energy, a vibrant current flowing between us, a silent affirmation of the spark I sought to rekindle. Her eyes, when they met mine in the rearview, held a newfound daring, a recognition of the intoxicating freedom that had begun to unfurl within her. This journey was awakening something primal in her, a wildness I both craved and knew would challenge us profoundly.

Mark, riding just behind us, maintained a steady, almost watchful presence, his eyes often drawn to Sarah's swaying form. I imagined the silent battle raging within him, the constant push and pull between his loyalty to me and the undeniable pull of his long-held desires. His face, usually a mask of quiet resolve, occasionally betrayed a flicker of something deeper, a yearning that spoke volumes without a single word. He was a man of discipline, yet even discipline had its limits when faced with such potent allure. The highway, with its ceaseless motion, seemed to amplify these unspoken tensions, making the air between us thick with unaddressed emotions. His struggle, a silent undercurrent, added another layer of complexity to our shared adventure.

David, ever the conversationalist, pulled alongside, his voice cutting through the wind, 'This is what life's all about, isn't it, Maverick? No nagging, no spreadsheets, just the roar and the road.' He winked, a clear jab at his own domestic woes, his need for uninhibited freedom evident in every word. 'And some damn fine scenery,' he added, his gaze sweeping over Sarah before settling back on me with a playful smirk. His casual flirtatiousness, while harmless on the surface, served as a constant reminder of Sarah's undeniable appeal, a subtle provocation that kept the underlying tension alive. He was the unburdened spirit, pushing the boundaries with a lightheartedness that belied the deeper currents at play.

As the sun dipped lower, painting the sky in fiery hues of orange and purple, our formation tightened, a cohesive unit against the vast expanse. The camaraderie was palpable, a shared bond forged in the crucible of the open road, yet beneath it pulsed a complex web of unspoken desires and loyalties. Each glance, each shared smile, each subtle shift in position, carried an unspoken weight, a silent acknowledgment of the unique dynamic we now embodied. The highway, once a symbol of simple freedom, had become a conduit for deeper currents, leading us not just across miles, but into the uncharted territories of our own hearts. It was a journey where every turn promised to reveal more than just a new vista.

The road ahead beckoned, a winding path promising both exhilaration and unforeseen challenges, leading us further from the familiar and deeper into the thrilling unknown. We were no longer just friends on a trip; we were protagonists in an unfolding drama, each heartbeat syncing with the powerful rhythm of our machines. The 'Forbidden Trail' was not yet in sight, but its shadow already stretched long before us, a tantalizing whisper of the boundaries we were destined to explore. This ride was a gamble, a high-stakes play for renewed passion and rediscovered intimacy, where the thrill of the forbidden might just be the ultimate aphrodisiac. The highway unfurled, revealing not just a path, but a destiny, beckoning us towards a night where loyalties would be tested and desires redefined.

Mark's Harley rumbled beneath him, a familiar, comforting growl that usually drowned out the noise in his head. Today, however, even the roar of the engine couldn't silence the insistent whisper of a name: Sarah. For years, he'd carried this secret, a silent, burning ember in his chest, carefully banked beneath layers of loyalty and friendship to Jake, his best friend. Now, with Sarah riding just ahead, her form swaying gracefully with every curve of the highway, that ember threatened to ignite into a full-blown inferno. This trip, Jake's grand idea to reignite his marriage, felt like a cruel joke on Mark's carefully constructed composure. He gripped the handlebars tighter, the leather warm beneath his calloused hands, a futile attempt to rein in the wild thoughts galloping through his mind.

He watched Jake, effortlessly cool on his own machine, oblivious to the silent battle raging just a few feet behind him. Jake, the charismatic leader and entrepreneur, was always able to get what he wanted, including Sarah. Mark had always admired Jake, their bond forged over countless miles and shared adventures, but a bitter taste often coated his tongue when his friend spoke of his wife with such casual ownership. It was a dark, ugly corner of his soul, one he rarely allowed himself to visit, yet Sarah's vibrant presence on this journey had thrown open the door to that forbidden room. He knew the rules, the unspoken code of brotherhood, and breaking them meant shattering everything.

Sarah, Jake's 'Vixen,' was a vision in the sunlight, her leather vest hugging curves that haunted Mark's dreams. Her hair, usually a cascade of wild curls, was tamed by the wind beneath her helmet, but he knew the spark in her eyes, the easy, captivating smile that could disarm any man. He imagined the way her full breasts would strain against the fabric, the tantalizing sway of her hips as she walked, a body that promised untold pleasures, a mind that was sharp and witty. She possessed that rare combination of innocence and raw sensuality that had captivated him from the moment he first saw her, a beauty that seemed to defy the very concept of aging. His gaze lingered, a silent, illicit caress.

The open road, usually his sanctuary, now felt like an accomplice to his burgeoning desires. Each mile brought them closer, not just physically, but emotionally, stripping away the everyday facades. The freedom of the ride, the wind whipping past, seemed to loosen the constraints on his own desires, whispering temptations he'd spent years trying to ignore. He felt an almost primal urge to break formation, to pull alongside her, to simply look into her eyes without the filter of Jake's presence. This journey was supposed to be about rekindling Jake and Sarah's spark, but for Mark, it was igniting a fire he might never be able to extinguish.

The internal conflict gnawed at him, a relentless ache in his chest. Loyalty to Jake, a bond forged in steel, warred with a longing for Sarah that was as old as time itself. He prided himself on his self-control, his stoic exterior, but Sarah's proximity was a constant, exquisite torture, eroding his resolve with every passing mile. He knew the dangers of this path, the destruction it could wreak on their friendships, on Jake's marriage, and on his own soul. Yet, a part of him, a rebellious, desperate part, wondered what it would be like to simply let go, to chase the forbidden thrill that pulsed beneath his skin.

Sometimes, a quick glance in his mirror would catch her eye, a flicker of a smile, a shared moment of the road's exhilaration. In those fleeting seconds, he imagined a different world, one where their eyes held a deeper understanding, a mutual recognition of an unspoken current. He knew she saw him as a friend, Jake's loyal shadow, but he hoped, foolishly perhaps, that a hint of his adoration, a whisper of his desire, might somehow breach the carefully constructed walls between them. The thought was dangerous, intoxicating, a forbidden fruit dangling just out of reach.

As they approached the turn-off for the 'Forbidden Trail,' a shiver ran down Mark's spine, not from the cool air, but from a profound sense of foreboding and excitement. David had spoken of the trail's wildness, its isolation, a place where rules blurred and inhibitions might fall away. Mark sensed this detour was more than just a challenging ride; it was a metaphor for the journey they were all unknowingly embarking on, a path into uncharted emotional territory. He wondered what secrets the trail would force them to confront, what desires it would unleash.

His heart hammered against his ribs, a drumbeat echoing the rhythm of his Harley. He was a man of discipline, a former military man who valued order, yet here, on this open road with Sarah so tantalizingly close, he felt utterly out of control. The thrill of the forbidden, the potent mix of danger and desire, was a powerful aphrodisiac, one he was struggling desperately to resist. This trip was pushing boundaries, not just for Jake and Sarah, but for him, forcing him to confront the deepest, most dangerous longings he had ever known, desires that could shatter everything.

The relentless roar of Jake's Harley, a rhythmic pulse beneath her, began to strip away Sarah's initial reservations, replacing them with an exhilarating sense of liberation. The wind whipped through her hair, a wild caress against her skin, and for the first time in what felt like years, she felt truly alive, unburdened by the mundane routines that had slowly dulled the vibrant edges of her marriage. Each mile dissolved a layer of polite inhibition, revealing a deeper current of adventurous spirit she had long kept carefully concealed. She leaned into Jake's broad back, but her gaze was forward, scanning the horizon, not just for the road ahead, but for the untamed possibilities it promised.

As the miles blurred, Sarah became acutely aware of the subtle shifts in the group's dynamic, particularly the heightened attention she commanded. Mark's quiet intensity, usually reserved, now seemed to hum with an unspoken current whenever their eyes met in the rearview mirror, a deep, possessive warmth that was both unsettling and undeniably thrilling. David's playful glances, his easy smile, carried a frank appreciation that made her pulse quicken in a way Jake's familiar gaze hadn't in ages. It was a potent cocktail of admiration, a recognition of her beauty that went beyond the comfortable confines of being 'Jake's wife,' and she found herself subtly, almost unconsciously, responding to it.

A delicious, forbidden tremor began to stir within her, a realization that this trip was not merely about rekindling Jake's passion, but about igniting her own dormant desires. The 'hot wife' persona Jake often playfully attributed to her started to feel less like a role and more like an inherent, powerful part of her being, a force she had perhaps underestimated. She grappled with the intoxicating allure of this newfound attention, a silent battle between her unwavering loyalty to Jake and the tantalizing pull of the unknown, of desires that felt exhilaratingly unscripted.

Instead of deflecting the charged atmosphere, Sarah found herself leaning into it, a confident smile playing on her lips as she occasionally caught Mark's intense stare or David's knowing wink. It wasn't an act of betrayal, but an exploration of her own sensuality, a reclaiming of a vibrant part of herself that had been subtly overshadowed by years of comfortable routine. This wasn't about seeking validation from others, but about acknowledging the potent power she possessed, a power that made her feel more alive, more desirable, than she had felt in a very long time.

She began to subtly challenge Jake's assumptions, not with words, but with a newfound assertiveness in her posture and her gaze. This was not just *his* adventure to reignite *their* passion; it was *her* journey too, and she was no longer content to be a passive passenger. She wanted to explore, to feel, to experience everything this 'forbidden ride' had to offer, on her own terms. The thought sparked a rebellious thrill deep within her, a silent promise to herself that this trip would be transformative, not just for their marriage, but for her own understanding of desire.

The anticipation of the 'Forbidden Trail,' whispered about in hushed, excited tones, amplified her growing confidence, painting vivid pictures of secluded spots and uncharted territories. 'The Oasis' Motel, the final destination, no longer felt like a mere resting place but a stage set for a culmination of all these simmering emotions and unspoken desires. Sarah realized she wasn't just along for the ride; she was an active participant, ready to embrace the thrill of the unknown, her adventurous spirit now fully awakened and demanding its due.

Her movements, once reserved, now carried a confident fluidity, a subtle swing in her hips as she dismounted her Harley, a playful tilt of her head when she spoke. The leather of her jacket felt like a second skin, accentuating the curves she had once taken for granted, now acutely aware of the appreciative glances it garnered. There was an undeniable magnetism to her presence, a quiet strength that emanated from her, signaling a woman who was no longer just observing the adventure, but fully embodying it.

The audacious 'Let's Roll' attitude, a phrase Jake often used to describe her adventurous spirit, now resonated deeply within her, no longer a mere reflection of his enthusiasm but a genuine expression of her own burgeoning desire for excitement. She was ready, truly ready, for whatever lay ahead on this thrilling, unpredictable journey. The open road had not just led them to new landscapes, but to a profound awakening within Sarah herself, leaving her poised on the edge of a new, exhilarating understanding of intimacy and desire.

David 'Rider' Chen, with his easy grin and eyes that seemed to dance with an unspoken challenge, was a natural instigator, a playful provocateur who could stir the pot without ever appearing malicious. His average build belied a core of lean strength, and his agility on his Harley was matched only by his quick wit. He fit seamlessly into the group, a newer addition to Jake and Mark's long-standing friendship, yet he carried an air of familiar camaraderie, always ready with a quip or an observation that cut right to the heart of the unspoken.

As their Harleys ate up the scenic highway, the wind whipping through their hair, David's voice, a casual counterpoint to the roaring engines, drifted back to Sarah. "Still living up to that 'Vixen' moniker, I see, Sarah," he called out, his tone light but with an appreciative glint in his eyes that was impossible to miss. "Not many women could make a leather vest look quite so... inviting." Jake, riding just ahead, caught the tail end of the comment and chuckled, a possessive pride stirring within him, even as a flicker of something more primal, a competitive edge, began to sharpen.

Later, during a brief stop for gas, David leaned against his bike, stretching casually as he spoke to Jake, his voice dropping just low enough for Sarah to catch snippets. "Man, you're a lucky bastard, Jake, getting to ride with such a stunning co-pilot." He sighed dramatically, a theatrical roll of his eyes. "Some of us are stuck in the desert, if you know what I mean. Lisa's been on a self-imposed celibacy kick for months, leaving a man to wonder if he's forgotten how to be a husband, or just a man at all." The raw honesty, though delivered with a laugh, resonated with a deeper frustration that was unmistakable.

Sarah, initially feigning disinterest, found herself drawn to his candor, a stark contrast to Mark's brooding silence. She offered a sympathetic smile, a silent acknowledgment of his plight, which David met with a knowing wink. "The open road, Sarah," he mused, his gaze lingering on her, "has a way of liberating desires, doesn't it? Makes you remember what it feels like to truly live, to truly want." Her 'Let's Roll' attitude, usually reserved for Jake, seemed to extend an unspoken invitation to the charged atmosphere he was so effortlessly creating.

Mark, riding a short distance behind, watched the exchange with a familiar tightening in his chest. David's easy charm, his blatant appreciation for Sarah, was a mirror to his own suppressed desires, amplifying the ache he constantly fought to hide. He gripped the handlebars tighter, the leather creaking under his knuckles, a silent battle raging within him to maintain his composure and loyalty amidst David's casual, yet potent, provocations.

Jake, while outwardly amused by David's antics, felt a complex mix of emotions swirling beneath his confident exterior. Part of him basked in the reflected glow of David's admiration for Sarah, a validation of his wife's undeniable allure. Yet, another part, a more primal instinct, recognized the subtle challenge, the unspoken question of boundaries that David's playful flirtations introduced. He was pushing for excitement, but David was pushing the line, testing the very limits of Jake's carefully constructed marital adventure.

David's seemingly innocent remarks and appreciative glances were not just idle banter; they were carefully placed stones, each one contributing to the path leading deeper into uncharted territory. He was an observer, yes, but also a catalyst, his less inhibited approach chipping away at the conventional veneers of friendship and marital commitment. His presence ensured that the undercurrents of desire, already simmering, would soon boil over, making the road trip far more volatile than any of them had initially anticipated.

As the sun began its slow descent, painting the sky in fiery hues, David gestured ahead to a barely visible turn-off. "Alright, Maverick," he called out, his voice laced with an almost mischievous glee, "This is it. The 'Forbidden Trail' awaits. Let's see what kind of desires this little detour unleashes." His words hung in the air, a playful challenge that promised an exhilarating descent into the very heart of their unspoken desires, an adventure that would test loyalties and redefine intimacy.

The relentless drone of the highway, a steady pulse against the vast expanse of open country, had begun to lull some of the initial excitement into a comfortable rhythm. Jake, however, felt a different kind of thrumming beneath his leather-clad chest, a restless anticipation that mirrored the powerful engine between his legs. His eyes, ever scanning the horizon for the next thrill, caught a subtle, almost imperceptible break in the dense foliage ahead, a sliver of darkness promising a deviation from their charted course. This was it, the moment he'd been building towards, the literal and metaphorical turn onto the path less traveled, where their carefully constructed world might just unravel in the most exhilarating way.

A knowing smirk tugged at Jake's lips as he signaled, his hand a confident gesture inviting them all to follow him into the unknown. This 'Forbidden Trail' wasn't merely a detour; it was a deliberate act, a calculated risk designed to strip away the mundane layers of their lives and expose the raw, untamed passion he yearned to reignite with Sarah. He imagined the dust clinging to her sun-kissed skin, the wildness in her eyes as they navigated the rough terrain together, a primal dance that would surely translate into a deeper, more carnal connection later. The thought alone sent a familiar, insistent rumble through his groin, confirming his instincts were precisely on track.

The entrance to the trail was an unassuming cut, a mere suggestion of a path swallowed by overgrown brush and shaded by ancient, gnarled oaks. It looked forgotten, untamed, a stark contrast to the smooth, predictable asphalt they were leaving behind. Sunlight dappled through the canopy, creating a kaleidoscope of shifting shadows that danced across the dirt track, hinting at secrets held close. This was no manicured route; it was a challenge, a test of skill and nerve, and its very wildness promised an escape from the constraints of their ordinary existence, a perfect stage for the extraordinary.

Sarah, initially observing the narrow, winding path with a flicker of apprehension, felt an unexpected jolt of excitement course through her. The air, suddenly cooler and tinged with the scent of damp earth and pine, seemed to whisper promises of adventure, awakening a dormant wildness within her. Her beautiful breasts, usually confined by more conventional attire, felt freer beneath her biker vest, a subtle rebellion against the expected. She glanced back at Jake, a mischievous glint in her eyes, a silent acknowledgment that she was ready to embrace whatever thrilling, perhaps even illicit, experiences this forbidden journey might offer, her 'Vixen' spirit stirring.

Mark's grip on his handlebars tightened, his gaze fixed on Sarah's lithe form as she expertly maneuvered her bike behind Jake. The sight of her, framed by the wild entrance to the trail, ignited a familiar, searing ache in his chest, a longing he perpetually fought to suppress. This secluded path, shrouded in mystery, felt like a physical manifestation of his own forbidden desires, a place where the thin veil of propriety might finally tear. He could already feel the heavy weight of temptation pressing down on him, his loyalty to Jake battling fiercely with the raw, visceral pull he felt towards his friend's stunning wife, his smile around her a mask for deeper emotions.

David, ever the pragmatist with an eye for opportunity, grinned broadly as Jake veered off the main road. He had been the one to suggest this particular 'Forbidden Trail,' knowing its reputation for seclusion and the exhilarating challenge it presented. The thought of escaping the monotony of his own marital frustrations, especially the sexual drought he'd endured for months, filled him with a potent sense of liberation. He admired Sarah's confident posture on her bike, openly appreciating her captivating beauty, already imagining the playful provocations he could unleash in such an isolated setting, a tantalizing prospect after so much deprivation.

As their Harleys rumbled onto the unpaved track, the change was immediate and palpable. The steady roar of the highway receded, replaced by the crunch of tires on gravel and the deeper, more resonant thrum of engines working harder. Dust plumed behind them, creating a hazy, golden shroud that seemed to detach them from the world they knew. The close quarters on the narrow trail intensified every interaction, every glance, every unspoken thought. The air crackled with a new, charged energy, the dynamic between the three men and one very attractive wife shifting irrevocably, shedding the last vestiges of conventional restraint.

The bikes bucked and swayed over roots and rocks, demanding their full attention, yet the heightened focus only sharpened their awareness of each other. Sarah's laughter, a bright, clear sound, drifted back to them as she leaned into a turn, her body fluid and graceful. Jake watched her, a possessive pride mingling with a dangerous curiosity, while Mark's eyes lingered, burning with an unacknowledged yearning. David, meanwhile, took in the entire scene with an almost clinical appreciation, a connoisseur of unfolding human drama, wondering how far this exhilarating ride would push them all past their comfort zones. The trail was leading them deeper, not just into the woods, but into themselves.

Harley Babe

Chapter 3

The Forbidden Trail

The growl of Maverick's Harley, a low, guttural rumble, vibrated through the worn floorboards of the 'Midnight Run' Bar, a primal symphony that announced our departure. Outside, the chrome glinted under the fading afternoon sun, reflecting the anticipation etched onto our faces. This was no ordinary ride; it was an expedition into the heart of desire, a calculated risk Jake had meticulously orchestrated to inject a much-needed spark back into his marriage with Sarah. What began as a plan for a double-date escape had, by a twist of fate a sick wife, an unattached friend morphed into an intoxicating equation: three men, one captivating woman, and the open road stretching into the unknown. The very thought of it, the raw, unadulterated potential, sent a familiar shiver of excitement down my spine, a deep-seated rumble mirroring the engine beneath me.

Jake, ever the charismatic leader, exuded an almost palpable aura of confident masculinity, his well-built frame a testament to years of embracing life's more audacious challenges. He had always approached his business ventures with a penchant for high stakes, and now, that same audacious spirit was being applied to the most intimate corners of his personal life. His internal monologue, usually a confident stream of strategy and ambition, now swirled with a deeper, almost vulnerable yearning to reconnect with Sarah, to rediscover the fervent passion he knew lay beneath the comfort of their routine. This trip, he believed, was not merely a journey across asphalt but a deliberate plunge into the thrilling depths of their shared intimacy, a gamble he was determined to win.

Sarah, his stunning wife, stood beside her bike, a vision of captivating allure, her beautiful breasts and perfectly sculpted ass accentuated by her adventurous, 'Let's Roll' demeanor. Initially, a flicker of hesitation had crossed her expressive features, a silent acknowledgment of the trip's inherent intensity, yet a profound curiosity for the promise of rekindled passion tugged at her. Her intelligent gaze swept over the three men, a subtle awareness of their collective attention, a potent blend of apprehension and burgeoning excitement simmering beneath her ever-present smile. She possessed the body of a young, attractive woman, undeniably, but it was coupled with the sharp mind and discerning sensibility of a middle-aged wife, a formidable combination poised on the brink of self-discovery.

Mark 'Rebel' Johnson, tall, slim, and undeniably well-endowed, leaned against his own gleaming Harley, his brooding intensity a stark contrast to Jake's boisterous enthusiasm. A long-time friend of Jake's, Mark's stoic exterior belied a deeply ingrained, secretly harbored desire for Sarah, a silent yearning that had simmered for years beneath the surface of their camaraderie. Every interaction with her was a careful dance, his eyes, though always accompanied by a smile in her presence, holding a depth of longing that threatened to betray his carefully constructed facade of loyalty. This trip, he knew, would test the very limits of his self-control, forcing him to confront the forbidden impulses he had so diligently suppressed.

Then there was David 'Rider' Chen, the newest addition to their tight-knit circle, his easy-going flirtatiousness a natural counterpoint to Mark's reserved intensity. David, of average build but surprisingly agile, openly appreciated Sarah's striking beauty, his gaze lingering with a playful, uninhibited admiration. His own marital frustrations, particularly a long-standing sexual drought with his absent wife, Lisa, had left him in a state of perpetual horniness, a restless energy that made him a natural catalyst for pushing boundaries. He was less concerned with forbidden love and more with the thrill of the moment, the camaraderie, and the unbridled freedom the road offered as an escape from his domestic woes.

As the engines roared to life, a palpable charge settled over the quartet. The unspoken dynamic of three eager men and one very attractive wife, Sarah 'Vixen' Riley, became overtly apparent, a delicious tension that crackled in the air. This was more than just a motorcycle trip; it was a deliberate foray into a landscape where the lines between friendship and desire blurred, where societal norms were left in the dust, replaced by the raw, intoxicating allure of the forbidden. The road, a ribbon of asphalt unspooling before them, promised not just scenic vistas but an escape from the mundane, an invitation to explore the untamed territories of their own hearts.

Pulling out of the 'Midnight Run' Bar, the thrum of their Harleys vibrating in unison, the scenic highway route unfolded, a winding path through picturesque countryside that promised both breathtaking beauty and isolated stretches. This was the chosen route, specifically selected for its sense of unbridled freedom and the potential for unexpected encounters, far from the critical gaze of everyday life. Each turn in the road felt like a step further into an uncharted emotional landscape, a deliberate move towards the 'Forbidden Trail' that David had hinted at a less-traveled, off-road path known only to a select few, symbolizing the deeper, more intimate journey they were about to embark upon.

The collective anticipation was a living entity, a low hum beneath the roar of the engines. Jake's hope for rekindled passion with Sarah was a driving force, while Sarah herself felt a burgeoning curiosity, a readiness to explore her own sensual agency. Mark's suppressed longing for Sarah became a silent battle waged within his stoic exterior, and David's uninhibited thrill for the adventure and the sensual possibilities infused the group with a playful, yet potent, energy. Each mile closer to their destination, 'The Oasis' Motel, heightened the individual desires simmering beneath the surface, preparing them for a night where inhibitions might finally give way.

The distant promise of 'The Oasis' Motel, a slightly seedy haven of anonymity along the highway, loomed large in their minds, the ultimate stage for the trip's escalating tensions. It was there, in the close quarters of a single motel room, that unspoken desires would likely be confronted, loyalties tested, and the true meaning of intimacy redefined. Diving into this unknown, both literally down the winding roads and metaphorically into the uncharted territory of their relationships, was a thrilling, dangerous prospect. The journey had just begun, and the thrill of the forbidden was already a potent, irresistible current pulling them all deeper into its intoxicating embrace.

The roar of the Harleys swallowed the mundane world, replacing it with a symphony of chrome and raw power as Jake 'Maverick' Riley led the charge down the scenic highway. Sarah 'Vixen' Riley clung to his back, her curves pressing against him, a constant, intoxicating reminder of the passion he sought to reignite. The wind whipped through their hair, a primal sensation that promised freedom and hinted at the uncharted territories they were about to explore. Jake glanced in his mirror, catching sight of Mark 'Rebel' Johnson and David 'Rider' Chen riding close behind, their eyes, he knew, often drifting to Sarah. The rumble in his groin wasn't just the engine; it was the heady mix of adventure and the thrill of sharing his beautiful wife with the open road and his closest friends.

Sarah felt the familiar hum of the engine beneath her, a vibration that resonated deep within her core, stirring a sense of wildness she often kept caged. The initial apprehension about this trip had faded, replaced by an exhilarating rush as the landscape blurred around them. She was acutely aware of the men behind them; a subtle shift in the air, a phantom touch, told her their gazes lingered. Mark's quiet intensity always felt like a warm blanket, while David's playful energy was a jolt of electricity. This journey wasn't just about Jake's desires; it was rapidly becoming an awakening for her own, a realization of the potent power she held, a power she was only just beginning to understand.

Mark 'Rebel' Johnson rode with a stoic facade, but his internal landscape was a tumultuous storm. Sarah's laughter, carried on the wind, was a cruel siren song, pulling at the threads of his loyalty to Jake. His eyes, despite his best efforts, were drawn to her, to the way her hair danced, to the curve of her back pressed against his best friend. The close quarters of the highway, the shared intimacy of the ride, were a torment and a temptation. Every mile was a battle, a silent war waged against years of suppressed longing, and he knew, with a sinking certainty, that this trip would push him to his absolute limits.

David 'Rider' Chen, ever the pragmatist with a mischievous glint in his eye, found himself enjoying the unfolding drama. His own marital frustrations, particularly Lisa's months-long sexual embargo, made the charged atmosphere around Sarah all the more intriguing. He rode alongside, occasionally catching Sarah's eye with a knowing smile, his appreciation for her undeniable. This trip was an escape, a breath of fresh air from his suffocating home life, and he wasn't above fanning the flames of desire, if only to feel the warmth of excitement again. The open road, he mused, was a confessional and a playground, all rolled into one.

A brief stop for gas at a roadside diner only intensified the unspoken currents flowing between them. Sarah, stretching gracefully, drew every eye, her 'Let's Roll' attitude radiating a vibrant energy. Jake's hand found the small of her back, a subtle claim, but his gaze swept over Mark and David, a challenge and an invitation. Mark's jaw tightened imperceptibly, his eyes lingering a moment too long on Sarah's bare midriff beneath her cropped top. David, however, simply grinned, offering Sarah a bottle of water with a wink that spoke volumes, acknowledging the delicious tension hanging in the air.

Jake felt a surge of pride, a possessive thrill, watching his wife command attention. This was precisely what he'd envisioned, the raw, undeniable attraction she exuded, amplified by the presence of his friends. He wanted to see her desired, to feel the edge of that forbidden excitement, believing it would reignite their own spark. The 'hot wife' dynamic, he realized, wasn't just about her; it was about him, about pushing his own boundaries, about daring to dance on the precipice of what was acceptable, all in the name of a deeper, more exhilarating passion.

Sarah, though outwardly composed, felt the heat of their collective gazes, a palpable energy that both unnerved and electrified her. She caught Mark's intense stare, a silent plea in his eyes, and then David's playful, almost conspiratorial glance. It was a potent cocktail of admiration and longing, and it awakened something dormant within her, a sensual awareness that hummed beneath her skin. This wasn't just a road trip; it was an exploration of her own power, a journey into the depths of her desires, making her question the comfortable confines of her marriage and what she truly craved.

As they remounted their bikes, David leaned in towards Jake, his voice a low, teasing murmur over the thrum of the engines. 'The open road has a way of loosening inhibitions, doesn't it, Maverick? What happens out here, stays out here.' His eyes flickered to Sarah, then to Mark, a knowing glint hinting at the delicious possibilities. David's words were a match to the tinder, pushing the boundaries of their unspoken agreement, laying bare the potential for transgression without ever explicitly stating it, a true catalyst for the forbidden encounters yet to come.

Mark's grip on his handlebars tightened, his knuckles white against the chrome. David's casual remark, aimed squarely at the simmering tension, felt like a deliberate provocation, a challenge to his self-control. He watched Sarah settle onto Jake's bike, her body a beacon of temptation, and the thought of David's easy flirtation, Jake's confident ownership, twisted a knot in his gut. His loyalty to Jake, once a steadfast anchor, now felt like a chain, binding him while his desires screamed for release. The road ahead, he knew, would offer no escape from this internal torment, only amplify it.

The sun began its slow descent, painting the sky in fiery hues that mirrored the escalating passions within the group. The miles melted away, bringing them closer to 'The Oasis' Motel, a destination that promised not rest, but a crucible for their desires. Each turn of the wheel, each shift of the gear, propelled them not just across the landscape, but deeper into the intoxicating allure of the forbidden. The close quarters of the day had set the stage, and the night ahead, in the privacy of a single motel room, held the promise of encounters that would redefine their relationships and challenge every boundary.

The roar of his Harley, usually a balm to Mark's restless soul, now served as a relentless drumbeat against the wall of his self-control. Every mile down the winding scenic highway, every shared glance in the rearview mirror, intensified the simmering conflict within him. He had spent years burying his feelings for Sarah beneath layers of loyalty to Jake, a friendship forged in the crucible of shared adventures and mutual respect. This trip, however, with its intoxicating freedom and Sarah's undeniable presence, was meticulously dismantling his carefully constructed defenses, one heart-thumping vibration at a time. The close quarters of their formation, with Sarah often just ahead or beside him, became a physical manifestation of the emotional proximity he struggled to deny, pushing his resolve to its breaking point.

Sarah, riding with Jake, was a vision of effortless allure, her vibrant energy practically radiating through the helmet. Her laughter, carried on the wind, was a melody that resonated deep within Mark, stirring desires he had long deemed forbidden. He watched the subtle sway of her hips as she navigated a curve, the way the sunlight caught her hair, and a potent cocktail of longing and guilt churned in his gut. Her playful spirit, usually a source of simple enjoyment, now felt like a direct challenge to his steadfast commitment to his best friend, making his internal landscape a treacherous terrain of unspoken wants and unyielding obligations.

Jake, oblivious to the silent battle raging beside him, exuded an easy confidence, his arm occasionally reaching back to touch Sarah's leg in a gesture of intimate ownership. That casual touch, a testament to their shared history and deep bond, was a dagger to Mark's already fractured peace. He valued Jake's friendship above almost all else, a bond forged in shared risks and unwavering trust, which made his own clandestine thoughts feel like the ultimate betrayal. The weight of that loyalty, a heavy anchor in the tempest of his desire, kept him tethered to a path he knew he had to follow, even as every instinct screamed for deviation.

As they veered off the main highway onto the 'Forbidden Trail,' a narrow, less-traveled path David had enthusiastically championed, the air grew thicker with unspoken tension. The secluded environment, hemmed in by ancient trees and dappled sunlight, felt like a stage set for illicit desires. When they paused at a small overlook, Sarah dismounted with a lithe grace, stretching her arms above her head, her movements fluid and captivating. Mark's gaze lingered, a silent, desperate prayer for strength battling the raw, primal urge to simply reach out and claim what his heart had always coveted, even knowing the catastrophic cost.

David, ever the instigator with his easy charm, only exacerbated Mark's internal turmoil. "Vixen's looking particularly radiant today, isn't she, fellas?" he'd quipped, his eyes twinkling as he winked at Sarah, then glanced pointedly at Mark. The casual observation, innocent on the surface, felt like a spotlight on Mark's deepest secret. He forced a strained smile, a practiced mask of nonchalance, while his pulse hammered a furious rhythm against his ribs. David's playful provocations, while seemingly harmless, chipped away at Mark's already fragile composure, making him question the very foundations of his self-control.

The journey continued, with each twist and turn of the trail serving as a metaphor for the labyrinthine path of Mark's own conscience. His hands gripped the handlebars, knuckles white, as if physically holding himself back from a precipice. He replayed conversations, scrutinizing Sarah's every smile, every touch, searching for a sign, a flicker of something that might justify his feelings, while simultaneously berating himself for even looking. The conflict was a relentless undertow, threatening to drag him beneath the surface of his carefully maintained decorum, leaving him gasping for air in the face of an impossible choice.

By the time they emerged from the 'Forbidden Trail,' dust-covered and exhilarated, Mark felt as though he had run a marathon, his emotional reserves utterly depleted. He had held the line, his loyalty to Jake, though tested, still intact. Yet, the victory felt hollow, a temporary reprieve rather than a true resolution. The raw, untamed desire for Sarah, far from being extinguished, had only been sharpened by the intense proximity and the constant battle of wills. He knew, with a chilling certainty, that this was merely the first skirmish in a war he might never truly win, a war that promised to redefine the very meaning of friendship and desire.

The roar of the Harley beneath Sarah 'Vixen' Riley was more than just an engine; it was a primal pulse, a resonant beat deep within her that had begun to quicken with each mile. She had started this journey with a flicker of apprehension, a familiar hesitancy about Jake's grand, sometimes impulsive, schemes to 'reignite' their passion. Yet, as the wind whipped through her hair and the scent of distant pine mingled with exhaust, a different kind of thrill, separate from Jake's intentions, started to blossom within her, hinting at a bolder, more uninhibited self.

She felt Mark's intense gaze on her in the rearview mirror, a familiar weight she'd long attributed to friendly admiration, but now, it carried a sharper edge, almost a palpable hunger. David, riding alongside, would occasionally offer a cheeky grin or a suggestive comment, his easy flirtation no longer just a playful distraction but a confirmation of her undeniable allure. This dual attention, once a source of mild discomfort, now sparked a peculiar sense of empowerment, a validation that stirred a long-dormant desire for more than just being admired.

As they veered onto the 'Forbidden Trail,' the familiar world receded, replaced by a dense canopy and winding, untamed paths that felt like a metaphor for her own awakening. The isolation, the challenge of the terrain, and the sheer audacity of the detour stripped away conventional inhibitions, allowing a raw, elemental part of her to surface. Each bump and curve of the trail was a physical reminder of the boundaries they were pushing, and Sarah found herself not just following, but actively leaning into the thrill, her body responding with an unexpected eagerness.

During a brief stop, Jake reached for her, his touch possessive yet a little too routine, a comfort she now found herself questioning. Instead of merely accepting his embrace, Sarah met his gaze, a new glint of challenge in her eyes, a silent question about the depth of their shared adventure. She initiated a playful squeeze of his hand, a subtle shift in their dynamic that hinted at her growing agency, a quiet assertion that this journey was as much about her desires as it was about his.

A dangerous spark ignited in her belly, a recognition of her own potent allure, not just for Jake, but for the hungry eyes that followed her, eyes that promised a different kind of excitement. She acknowledged the thrill of being desired by other men, a sensation that had always been present but carefully suppressed, now allowed to simmer and deepen. This forbidden awareness wasn't a betrayal, she rationalized, but an expansion, a vital exploration of her own sensuality, a testament to the fact that her desires were hers alone to discover.

She had always loved Jake, cherishing their bond, but this trip was peeling back layers, revealing a Sarah who craved more than just rekindled passion; she sought a raw, uninhibited expression of her own sensuality. The conventional lines of their marriage, once so clearly defined, began to blur, not in a destructive way, but in a manner that promised a more authentic, perhaps even more profound, connection. She realized that truly reigniting their passion meant not just meeting Jake's expectations, but fearlessly asserting her own.

Her smile, usually a default expression of politeness or affection, now held a knowing glint, a subtle challenge to the men around her, a silent invitation to engage with the woman she was becoming. She moved with a newfound confidence, her hips swaying a little more deliberately, her gaze lingering a fraction longer, a physical manifestation of her internal shift. Her adventurous attitude, once a playful persona, was now deeply ingrained, reflected in every subtle gesture and confident stride.

The thought of 'The Oasis' Motel no longer filled her with vague apprehension but with a thrilling anticipation, a sense of readiness for whatever the night might bring. It wasn't just a place to rest; it was a crucible, a stage where the unspoken desires and simmering tensions of the day would inevitably converge. Sarah envisioned it not as a passive recipient of Jake's plans, but as an active participant, a woman with her own desires, ready to shape the adventure.

Sarah was no longer merely Jake's wife, passively along for the ride; she was 'Vixen,' untamed and ready to claim the desires that had long simmered beneath the surface, to explore the intoxicating freedom of the open road and the open heart. Her agency had emerged, not as a defiant act, but as an undeniable force, setting the stage for a night where loyalties would be challenged and the true meaning of intimacy redefined on her own terms.

The sun dipped below the horizon, painting the sky in audacious hues of orange and purple, a fitting backdrop for the audacious turn their journey was taking. Jake 'Maverick' Riley felt the familiar thrum of his Harley beneath him, a powerful counterpoint to the accelerating beat of his own heart. He glanced at Sarah, her silhouette against the fading light, her hair a wild halo escaping her helmet, and a surge of primal satisfaction coursed through him. This trip, his meticulously planned gamble to infuse their marriage with a much-needed jolt of adrenaline and desire, was undeniably working, the air thick with an almost palpable anticipation.

Pulling into the gravel lot of 'The Oasis' Motel, Jake killed his engine, the sudden silence amplifying the hum of their collective excitement. He dismounted, a confident stride taking him to Sarah's side, his hand settling on the small of her back, a possessive yet inviting gesture. 'Looks like our little hideaway,' he murmured, his voice a low rumble meant only for her, his thumb tracing a suggestive circle just above her jeans. He knew the spark he sought wasn't just about the open road; it was about the raw, uninhibited intimacy only an adventure like this could truly unlock.

Sarah turned, her eyes sparkling with a mix of apprehension and undeniable allure, her smile a slow, knowing curve. 'Our 'oasis' indeed, Maverick,' she replied, her voice a sultry whisper that sent a shiver down his spine. She leaned into his touch, a silent acknowledgment of the unspoken desires that had been simmering between them, and within the group, all day. Her gaze flickered briefly to Mark and David, who were already dismounting their own bikes, a subtle shift in her posture hinting at the complex dance of attraction she was navigating.

Mark, ever the stoic observer, caught the fleeting exchange, a muscle twitching in his jaw as he watched Jake's hand linger on Sarah. His own desires, long suppressed, felt like a raw wound in the charged atmosphere, each playful touch or suggestive glance from Jake a fresh stab. He forced a casual smile, but his eyes, dark and intense, betrayed the simmering jealousy that threatened to boil over. This 'adventure' was pushing his loyalty to Jake to its absolute limit, challenging every boundary he had meticulously constructed around his feelings for Sarah.

David, ever the pragmatist with a mischievous glint, sauntered over, his gaze sweeping over the group with an almost professional assessment. 'Well, isn't this cozy,' he quipped, a knowing smirk playing on his lips, 'one room, three bikes, and one very stunning Vixen.' His comment, seemingly light-hearted, was a deliberate flick of the match, igniting the already volatile mixture of desire and camaraderie. He ran a hand through his hair, a subtle gesture of his own underlying frustration, a silent testament to the marital drought he'd been enduring.

Jake met David's gaze, a challenging grin spreading across his face. 'Cozy is an understatement, Rider,' he retorted, pulling Sarah closer, his arm now firmly around her waist. 'Tonight, we redefine cozy.' He looked at Sarah, his eyes burning with an almost predatory intensity, telegraphing his intent to her with an unspoken promise of unbridled passion. The notion of the single room wasn't just a logistical convenience; it was a deliberate, provocative choice, a stage set for the ultimate marital rekindling.

The motel room, though basic, felt charged with an almost electric energy, the air thick with unspoken expectations. Jake's plan, initially a simple quest for renewed intimacy, had evolved into something far more audacious, a thrilling tightrope walk between marital passion and the intoxicating thrill of shared, almost forbidden, desire. He watched Sarah move, her easy confidence and natural allure captivating not just him, but undeniably, his friends as well. The 'hot wife' persona, his initial catalyst, was now a living, breathing force, captivating everyone.

He felt a delicious tremor of excitement, a potent mix of anticipation and a hint of nervous thrill. This wasn't just about him and Sarah anymore; it was about embracing the raw, untamed spirit of the road, the freedom to explore desires that traditionally remained veiled. Jake knew he was pushing boundaries, not just for his marriage, but for their entire friendship dynamic, venturing into a territory where loyalties would be tested and the true meaning of intimacy, in its most expansive form, would be laid bare. The night had only just begun, promising revelations and passions that would forever alter their journey.

Chapter 4

The Oasis of Desire

The roar of their Harleys finally softened into a low rumble as the quartet pulled into the parking lot of 'The Oasis' Motel, a beacon of unassuming anonymity under the desert's fading light. Dust motes danced in the last rays of the sun, clinging to chrome and leather, a testament to the miles devoured and the adventures shared. This wasn't some high-end resort, but a functional, slightly seedy stopover, chosen precisely for its lack of pretense and promise of undisturbed privacy. The air, still warm from the day's ride, seemed to thicken with a different kind of heat now, one born of proximity and unspoken desires. Here, far from the city's judging eyes, the boundaries Jake so eagerly sought to push felt less like distant lines and more like the very walls of the motel itself.

Jake 'Maverick' Riley dismounted his bike with confident, almost predatory grace, his eyes immediately seeking Sarah. A primal satisfaction hummed through him; he had orchestrated this, brought them to this precipice. He watched her dismount, her movements fluid and captivating, a smile already playing on his lips as his gaze lingered on her form. Tonight was about rekindling, about reminding both of them of the scorching passion that still smoldered beneath the surface of their comfortable marriage. The open road had been the appetizer, but 'The Oasis' was where the main course would be served, a feast he intended to savor. His pulse quickened, anticipating the delicious tension that was about to unfold, knowing full well the eyes of his friends were also fixed on his stunning wife.

Sarah 'Vixen' Riley felt the weight of those gazes, a familiar warmth spreading through her as she slipped off her bike. Her initial hesitation about the trip's intensity had slowly dissolved, replaced by growing curiosity and thrilling sense of anticipation. The freedom of the ride had awakened something within her, a sensual current that now hummed beneath her skin. She glanced at Jake, then subtly at Mark and David, acknowledging the unspoken admiration in their eyes a power she was beginning to consciously wield. This wasn't just Jake's adventure; it was becoming hers, a journey into the exhilarating depths of her own desires. The motel room, plain as it appeared, felt charged with potent, almost dangerous energy, beckoning her to explore the edges of her own wildness.

Mark 'Rebel' Johnson, ever the brooding observer, parked his Harley with precise, almost ritualistic care, his gaze anything but detached. His eyes found Sarah instantly, a familiar ache tightening in his chest as he watched her move, utterly captivating. The day's ride had only intensified his long-held, unspoken feelings, each curve of the road mirroring the dangerous curves of her body that haunted his thoughts. Loyalty to Jake warred fiercely with desire that felt increasingly impossible to suppress in these close quarters. He offered a tight, polite smile, a mask he hoped was impenetrable, but inside, a storm brewed, threatening to break the carefully constructed dam of his self-control. This motel, this single room, felt less like an oasis and more like a crucible for his tortured affections.

David 'Rider' Chen, ever the pragmatic pleasure-seeker, swung off his bike with an easy grin, his eyes openly appreciating Sarah's undeniable allure. Unlike Mark, David made no secret of his admiration, his flirtatious nature a natural extension of his personality and current marital frustrations. He craved excitement, a release from the mundane, and this trip, with Sarah as its vibrant centerpiece, promised exactly that. His own wife, Lisa, had effectively cut off their sexual intimacy months ago, leaving him with simmering frustration that made any hint of pleasure intensely appealing. He reveled in the charged atmosphere, a playful instigator ready to fan the flames, intrigued to see just how far the boundaries would bend, or break. For David, this was less about deep emotional commitment and more about the exhilarating thrill of the moment, a much-needed escape.

As they gathered their overnight bags, a subtle shift occurred in the group dynamic. The easy camaraderie of the ride gave way to palpable tension, a shared awareness of the night's potential. Jake caught Sarah's eye, a possessive yet inviting glint within his gaze, a silent question passing between them. Mark's jaw tightened almost imperceptibly, his internal conflict a silent scream against the backdrop of the desert's quiet. David, ever the provocateur, offered a knowing smirk, his eyes dancing between Sarah and the two men, a clear signal that he was ready for whatever the night might bring. The unspoken hung heavy in the air, a thick, intoxicating perfume of anticipation. This wasn't just a rest stop; it was the designated arena for their desires.

The room itself was standard motel fare: two queen beds, a small table, a television that looked like it belonged to another decade. Yet, in this context, its very ordinariness made it extraordinary. It was a blank canvas upon which the night's desires would be painted, a stark stage for the unfolding drama. The single room, Jake's deliberate choice, eliminated any pretense of separation, forcing an intimacy that was both exciting and terrifying. Every rustle of clothing, every shared breath, would be amplified, creating an inescapable cocoon of heightened sensation. The air conditioning hummed, a thin, mechanical counterpoint to the racing heartbeats within the small space, promising a long, unforgettable night.

Once inside, a brief, almost comical moment of awkwardness settled over them as they dropped their bags and the small space felt even smaller. Jake, ever the leader, broke the silence with a light-hearted quip, but his eyes never left Sarah, a silent invitation in their depths. Sarah, in turn, felt a blush creep up her neck, a delicious warmth spreading through her as she met his gaze, then subtly, fleetingly, Mark's and David's. The initial barrier of polite distance began to crumble, replaced by charged energy that made the hairs on her arms stand on end. The first tentative steps into the 'one motel room adventure' had been taken, and the air crackled with the promise of what was to come.

The 'Forbidden Trail' they had ridden earlier that day wasn't merely a physical path; it was a metaphor, a prelude to this very moment. Now, within the confines of 'The Oasis' Motel, the true journey was about to begin, one that would delve into the uncharted territories of their relationships and desires. Jake's entrepreneurial spirit, his penchant for risk, had led them here, to the brink of an experience that promised to redefine intimacy. The stage was set, the players were ready, and the intoxicating allure hung heavy, a silent challenge to loyalties and an open invitation to explore the deepest, most primal corners of their hearts.

The rumble of their Harleys faded into the desert night as Jake killed the engine, the Oasis Motel sign flickering its tired neon promise of rest and secrecy. The place was shabby, but its shadows seemed to invite more than just sleep, as if the walls themselves knew what was coming. Sarah swung off her bike with grace that turned heads, her smile lighting the courtyard in a way no bulb could. Mark pulled in close behind, his gaze catching on her for a heartbeat longer than he meant before he looked away, the ache in his chest sharper than usual. David, practical as ever, had already gone to the front desk, though the playful spark in his eyes betrayed how well he understood the deeper game unfolding. The courtyard's wilting palms and peeling paint offered little charm, but the place felt charged, as though waiting to host a drama no one dared name aloud.

Sarah sensed it instantly. The road had been wild and freeing, but here the anticipation carried different weight, intimate and dangerous. She met Jake's proud, possessive look, then Mark's smoldering one, and finally David's open admiration. Any hesitation she'd felt about this trip had melted away. What stirred inside her now wasn't fear but curiosity, the thrill of realizing she wasn't just along for the ride she was its center. A quiet spark flared as she shed her helmet, the queen stepping onto the board with her own cards to play.

Jake watched her with satisfaction edged by unease. He had wanted this, the fire, the testing of limits, but Sarah's easy command of the space unsettled him. Mark's stiff posture, David's bold glances each detail sharpened Jake's resolve. He'd orchestrated this gamble, but now it was running hotter than expected, and the only way forward was through.

For Mark, discipline had always been armor. Years of burying his feelings for Sarah under loyalty to Jake had kept him steady. But the closeness of the motel stripped that armor thin. Every glance, every laugh was a reminder of what he wanted but could never have. The soldier in him held the line, but barely.

David, meanwhile, reveled in the spectacle. The tension was a show he couldn't look away from, colored by his own frustration at the emptiness waiting for him back home. Sarah's magnetism was obvious, and he didn't bother hiding his appreciation. "Looks like the Forbidden Trail isn't the only thing heating up, huh, Maverick?" he quipped, enjoying the ripple his words created.

The night grew heavier as they settled in. Bottles clinked, words dropped into silences that stretched too long. Sarah's laugh, bright and mischievous, only heightened the pull each man felt toward her. Jake's protective arm around her waist read as both claim and challenge. Mark's quiet restraint was loud in its own way, while David's banter pushed the tension further than anyone wanted to admit. The Oasis Motel, run-down and anonymous, had become a crucible. Whatever unfolded here would test not just loyalty but the limits of desire itself.

Sarah felt it too. The desert heat clung to her skin, but what burned brighter was the realization that she wasn't merely desired she was the one steering their every thought. Confidence threaded through her movements, her body speaking with a fluency that left no doubt she knew her power. She wasn't a bystander to this night. She was the flame they couldn't resist circling, and she intended to see just how close each of them was willing to come.

As they finally made their way toward the single motel room Jake had booked, the air thrummed with almost unbearable anticipation, each step laden with unspoken expectations. The communal courtyard, for all its open space, offered no escape from the intimate entanglement that awaited them behind the closed door. Jake's hand on the doorknob felt momentous, a gateway to a night that promised to redefine their relationships, for better or worse. Mark's jaw was clenched, his internal battle raging, while David's eyes sparkled with almost giddy excitement, a thrill-seeker ready for the ride. Sarah, however, walked with newfound confidence, a subtle sway in her hips that spoke of both apprehension and potent, eager curiosity. The silence that fell between them as the door creaked open was louder than any roar of a Harley, pregnant with the weight of impending decisions and desires. This wasn't just a room; it was the arena where their deepest longings would finally confront the light of day.

The air inside 'The Oasis' motel room felt thick, almost palpable, a stark contrast to the open road they had just conquered. Jake watched Sarah as she moved, her silhouette framed by the dim light filtering through the cheap curtains, every curve of her body a silent provocation. He had envisioned this moment, the culmination of their adventure, but the presence of Mark and David amplified the tension, turning a planned rekindling into a high-stakes gamble. A primal thrumming started deep within him, familiar anticipation that always preceded a boundary-pushing endeavor.

Jake's gaze lingered on Sarah, possessive warmth spreading through him, yet he couldn't ignore the subtle shifts in Mark's posture, the way David's eyes followed her every move. This trip was meant to reignite something between him and Sarah, to inject fire back into their marriage, but now it felt like a crucible for all their desires. He craved Sarah's touch, her uninhibited passion, but part of him also thrilled at the danger, the unspoken challenge of holding her attention amidst the hungry glances of his closest friends. The allure was undeniably intoxicating, and Jake felt a surge of both excitement and unsettling apprehension.

Sarah, for her part, felt the weight of their collective gazes, a sensation that was both unnerving and undeniably electrifying. The raw energy of the day, the roar of the Harleys, and the shared vulnerability on the 'Forbidden Trail' had chipped away at her reservations, leaving her exposed to a surge of her own untapped desires. She caught Mark's intense stare, then David's playful smirk, and a flush crept up her neck, a heady mix of embarrassment and burgeoning power. This wasn't just about Jake's vision of their marriage; it was becoming a journey into her own sensuality, a reawakening she hadn't anticipated.

Mark stood by the window, ostensibly looking out at nothing, but his reflection in the glass betrayed his true focus: Sarah. Every casual movement she made sent a jolt through him, an ache that had been festering for years now amplified to an unbearable degree. His loyalty to Jake, a bond forged over countless miles and shared adventures, felt stretched taut, threatening to snap under the weight of his potent longing. He wanted to look away, to douse the fire in his gut, but the magnetic pull of her presence in such close quarters was an irresistible force, a silent torment.

David, ever the pragmatist with a mischievous glint in his eyes, broke the heavy silence. He leaned against the doorframe, a casual smile playing on his lips. "Well, this is cozy," he drawled, his gaze sweeping over the three of them, lingering on Sarah. "Reminds me of a camping trip, only with less dirt and more... potential." His words, light as they were, landed with the impact of a thrown gauntlet, acknowledging the simmering tension and subtly pushing the boundaries, a playful instigator in the unfolding drama. He genuinely enjoyed the thrill, a welcome distraction from his own marital frustrations.

Jake shot David a look, a mix of warning and grudging appreciation for his audacity, then turned back to Sarah, a silent question in his eyes. Sarah met his gaze, a flicker of defiance and a spark of something untamed dancing within hers. She took a slow sip from her drink, her lips moist and full, then deliberately ran the tip of her tongue along the rim of the glass, a small, unconscious gesture that felt incredibly intimate and provocative in the charged atmosphere. The air crackled, the unspoken desires in the room solidifying into a palpable presence, daring them all to acknowledge it.

The simple act sent a jolt through all three men. Mark clenched his jaw, his internal battle raging, while David's smile widened, knowing appreciation in his eyes. Jake felt a surge of pride, a thrill at Sarah's burgeoning confidence, but also a sliver of unease. This was precisely the excitement he had hoped for, yet seeing her so openly desired, so utterly captivating, stirred a complex cocktail of emotions within him. The reckoning had begun, a moment where the thin veneer of normalcy was stripped away, revealing the raw, untamed desires beneath.

Sarah felt the shift in their collective energy, the intensity of the male gaze no longer daunting but empowering. She moved closer to Jake, her hand lightly brushing his arm, a subtle invitation that was meant for him, yet carried an undeniable ripple effect through the room. Her body hummed with newfound energy, a daring spirit that had been dormant for too long, now fully awake and ready to explore the thrilling, dangerous landscape of desire. She was no longer just Jake's wife; she was 'Vixen,' a woman embracing her own power.

Jake's hand instinctively covered hers, a silent claim, but his eyes darted to Mark, then David, a silent challenge passing between them. He had sought to reignite passion, to add a spark, but Sarah's response was proving more potent and unpredictable than he had imagined. This wasn't merely about his desires anymore; it was about her agency, her willingness to explore the edges of their relationship, and the dangerous dance they were all now entangled in. The thrill was no longer an abstract concept but a tangible, breathing entity in their small motel room.

As the night deepened, the silence stretched, punctuated only by the soft hum of the motel's ancient air conditioner and the rapid thumping of four hearts. Each person in the room was acutely aware of the others, of the unspoken needs and wants that pulsed beneath the surface. The 'A Night of Reckoning' was not just a title; it was a promise, a crucible where loyalties would be tested, boundaries shattered, and the true meaning of intimacy, in its most daring form, would finally be confronted. The stage was set for everything to unfurl.

The morning light, usually a herald of new beginnings, seemed to cast long, knowing shadows across the shared space of 'The Oasis' motel room, heavy with the residue of unspoken desires. A palpable tension, thicker than the lingering scent of stale coffee and faint perfume, hung in the air, a testament to the boundaries blurred and perhaps even breached during the long, restless hours. Each glance exchanged between Jake, Sarah, Mark, and David felt weighted, laden with the silent question of what had truly transpired and the implications for their interwoven lives. The easy camaraderie of the open road had given way to a precarious emotional landscape, where every breath seemed to hold a secret, every touch a potential revelation. Sarah, in particular, felt the collective gaze, a silent acknowledgment of her captivating allure that now felt less like a compliment and more like a challenge. The thrill Jake had sought to inject into their marriage had undeniably arrived, but it carried an intoxicating danger he was only just beginning to fully comprehend.

Jake 'Maverick' Riley, usually so quick with a joke or commanding decision, found his usual confidence tempered by an unfamiliar unease. He watched Sarah, her movements graceful yet subtly guarded, and a proprietary warmth mingled with a prickle of jealousy he hadn't anticipated. His grand design to rekindle their passion had perhaps succeeded too well, igniting not just their marital spark but also wildfire attractions he now struggled to contain within the confines of his own making. The glint in Mark's eyes when he looked at Sarah, the casual yet lingering appreciation in David's gaze, were no longer abstract observations but potent, undeniable forces threatening the very structure he cherished. This wasn't merely a risk; it was a high-stakes gamble with the most precious aspects of his life, and the thrill was rapidly morphing into perilous uncertainty.

Sarah 'Vixen' Riley, usually content to navigate social currents with charming smile, found herself acutely aware of the magnetic pull she exerted, a power she was only now truly beginning to harness. The previous night had stripped away layers of complacency, revealing not only her husband's fervent desire but also the raw, unadulterated longing in the eyes of their friends. She felt a delicious, almost dangerous surge of validation, recognition of her own sensuality that had long been dormant beneath the surface of their comfortable marriage. Yet, this newfound agency came with heavy weight, forcing her to confront the intricate web of loyalty and desire, and to question how far she was willing to let these currents carry her before the familiar shores of commitment became irrevocably distant.

Mark 'Rebel' Johnson, typically a bastion of stoic reserve, found his carefully constructed emotional walls crumbling under the relentless pressure of proximity and unspoken yearning. Every shared laugh, every accidental brush of hands, every lingering glance from Sarah felt like direct assault on his long-held secret, a desire he had painstakingly buried for years beneath layers of friendship and respect for Jake. His loyalty to his friend, a bond forged over countless miles and shared adventures, now felt like fragile shield against the overwhelming tide of his own attraction. He wrestled with gnawing guilt, fervent hope, and the terrifying prospect of shattering everything for a moment of desperate, exhilarating connection that might never be truly his.

David 'Rider' Chen, the group's light-hearted instigator, couldn't help but observe the palpable tension, finding perverse amusement in the unfolding drama even as he felt stirrings of his own unfulfilled desires. His marital frustrations with Lisa, particularly the prolonged sexual drought, made him particularly attuned to the raw hunger simmering beneath the surface of their polite interactions. He saw Sarah not just as Jake's wife, but as a vibrant, desirable woman, and his playful provocations, often cloaked in humor, served to subtly fan the flames. He was curious, detached observer, yet his very presence, his uninhibited appreciation of beauty and desire, acted as silent, potent catalyst, urging the others to confront their own deepest, most dangerous impulses.

The confrontation, when it came, wasn't sudden explosion of accusations but slow, simmering revelation, a series of loaded silences and pointed observations that stripped away the last vestiges of pretense. A seemingly innocuous comment from David about the 'excitement of the unknown' hung heavy in the air, drawing sharp glance from Jake and subtle blush from Sarah. Mark shifted uncomfortably, his eyes fixed on some distant point, yet his entire posture screamed of internal conflict. It was silent battle waged with glances and unspoken words, each participant acutely aware of the treacherous ground they now occupied, the unspoken desires now too potent to ignore or deny.

This delicate dance of confrontation didn't resolve anything; instead, it intensified the intoxicating thrill, elevating the stakes to almost unbearable degree. The previous night's blurred lines now seemed starkly defined, yet the allure of stepping over them felt stronger than ever. Jake, seeing the subtle shifts in Sarah's demeanor and the undeniable pull between her and his friends, felt primal mix of fear and strange, exhilarating curiosity. The boundaries of their marriage, once so solid, now felt fluid, inviting daring exploration that promised either profound renewal or irreversible fragmentation. The raw energy of their desires, unleashed on the open road, demanded a reckoning.

The group dynamic, once comfortable quartet of friends, had irrevocably transformed into something far more volatile and unpredictable. The easy laughter now carried an edge, the shared glances held deeper, more personal meaning, and the unspoken desires had become tangible, almost suffocating presence. This was no longer just a motorcycle trip; it had become a crucible, forging new connections while threatening to shatter old ones. The trail they had ridden, both literally and figuratively, had led them to a point of no return, a place where the rules of friendship and fidelity were being rewritten in the exhilarating, dangerous language of raw desire.

Yet, within this charged atmosphere, nascent understanding began to emerge, glimmer of the courage required to navigate this uncharted emotional territory. The confrontation, though unsettling, offered strange clarity, forcing each individual to look inward and acknowledge the complex interplay of passion, loyalty, and self-discovery. It became clear that to move forward, to truly rediscover intimacy, they would have to transcend the superficial thrill and delve into the deeper, more challenging aspects of their true desires. This was not merely about succumbing to temptation, but about embracing redefined, more honest form of connection, one that promised both vulnerability and unparalleled, exhilarating freedom.

The dawn at The Oasis Motel broke with strange, almost sacred quietude, stark contrast to the fervent energies that had pulsed through their shared space mere hours before. Jake lay beside Sarah, her warmth a palpable anchor, yet the air between them thrummed with unspoken reverberations, a tapestry woven from raw desires and newly acknowledged truths. The experience had peeled back layers of their conventional understanding, leaving them both exposed to deeper, more profound sense of self and shared vulnerability, an intimacy forged in the crucible of temptation and courage.

For Jake 'Maverick' Riley, the night had been seismic shift, forcing him to confront the superficiality of merely 'rekindling' a flame. He had sought excitement, a spark to reignite, but had instead stumbled into conflagration that demanded complete re-evaluation of his marriage. The thrill had indeed delivered adrenaline rush, yet it was the raw, unvarnished honesty it provoked that truly resonated, realization that genuine passion transcended mere physical acts, demanding emotional reciprocity and fearless exploration of boundaries.

Sarah 'Vixen' Riley, too, felt undeniable transformation stirring within her, awakening to her own potent agency. She had navigated the intoxicating currents of desire, not as passive object, but as woman fully in command of her sensuality, embracing the power that lay within her allure. The experience had not just reignited her passion for Jake; it had redefined her relationship with herself, empowering her to assert her desires and negotiate the terms of their intimacy, moving beyond the taken-for-granted into dynamic partnership of equals.

The ripple effects extended to Mark and David, who now moved with new, subtle deference, acknowledging the redefined landscape of their friendships. Mark 'Rebel' Johnson, ever the stoic, carried the weight of his unvoiced desires with newfound, almost melancholic grace, understanding that some lines, once blurred, could never be fully redrawn. David 'Rider' Chen, ever the pragmatic observer, seemed to glean deeper understanding of the complex emotional terrain, perhaps even reflecting on the barren stretches of his own marital landscape, the lack of passion starkly highlighted by the intensity he had witnessed.

The trail had not just been physical detour; it had been metaphorical descent into uncharted emotional territory, establishing new, unspoken accord among them all. The conventional norms of their lives had been tested, stretched, and in some ways, irrevocably altered, replaced by fluid understanding where loyalty was not simply about adherence to rules, but about honest engagement with the deepest parts of themselves and each other. They had collectively pushed the envelope, discovering that true intimacy often lay beyond the comfortable confines of expectation.

This was not merely about the thrill of transgression, but about the profound revelations it unearthed. The courage to explore had illuminated their deepest desires, fears, and the true resilience of their connections. It demonstrated that seeking excitement wasn't betrayal of commitment, but daring act of self-discovery that could, paradoxically, strengthen the bonds that mattered most, provided it was approached with honesty and willingness to confront uncomfortable truths.

As their Harleys roared to life once more, the journey back held different resonance, the scenic highway now a testament to their shared, altered reality. The wind whipping past them carried not just the scent of freedom, but the lingering echoes of confessions and unspoken understandings. The landscape, once backdrop for adventure, now mirrored the expansive, sometimes daunting, territory of their redefined relationships, a journey that continued long after the engines fell silent.

Jake and Sarah's marriage, stripped of its old routines and infused with this raw, potent honesty, felt both more fragile and infinitely stronger. They had confronted the shadows, danced with temptation, and emerged with more nuanced understanding of love one that embraced both comfort and chaos, fidelity and the wild, untamed spirit of desire. Their intimacy was no longer given but living, breathing entity, demanding constant attention, exploration, and brave willingness to venture into the unknown together.

The friendships, too, had settled into new equilibrium, marked by unspoken pact of shared secrets and deepened, albeit complex, loyalty. Mark's respect for Jake had grown, tinged with bittersweet knowledge of his own unfulfilled longings, while David carried new appreciation for the intricate dance of human connection, his flirtatious nature now underscored by subtle wisdom. They were forever bound by the experience, brotherhood forged not just on the road, but in the crucible of desire and vulnerability.

Ultimately, 'Redefining Intimacy' meant acknowledging that true connection was not static destination, but ongoing, exhilarating journey continuous exploration of self and other, demanding courage, honesty, and audacious embrace of all that lay beneath the surface. It was testament to the idea that passion, when genuinely sought and bravely confronted, could transcend societal expectations, transforming relationships into something richer, deeper, and infinitely more thrilling than they had ever dared to imagine.

Chapter 5

The Aftermath and the Ride Home

The first tendrils of dawn, weak and uncertain, crept through the gaps in the motel room's heavy drapes, casting long, distorted shadows across the rumpled sheets. A profound silence hung in the air, thick with the lingering scent of desire, a potent blend of shared skin, musky cologne, and the faint, sweet perfume of Sarah. Each breath felt charged, a silent acknowledgment of the intoxicating unraveling that had transpired within these walls, an intimate symphony played out under the cloak of night. The quiet hum of the air conditioner, a constant companion, now seemed to punctuate the profound stillness, marking the passage from unbridled passion to a dawn laden with new realities.

Sarah, stirring slowly, felt an unfamiliar yet exhilarating hum resonating deep within her, a vibrant echo of the night's audacious exploration. Her body, exquisitely sated, pulsed with a newfound awareness, a thrilling confirmation of desires she had long kept tethered, now gloriously unleashed. She traced the faint outline of an arm beside her, a gesture of quiet contemplation, her mind replaying fragments of the forbidden dance, acknowledging the courage it took to step into such uncharted territory. This journey, initially Jake's quest for rekindled excitement, had irrevocably become her own awakening, a powerful rediscovery of personal agency and unbridled sensuality.

Jake, rousing beside her, felt a primal satisfaction radiating from his core, a deep-seated thrum that resonated with the powerful roar of his Harley. He had sought to inject a much-needed spark, but the inferno they had collectively ignited last night had far surpassed all his carefully laid expectations, pushing boundaries he had only dared to glimpse. A flicker of possessiveness, an instinctual male urge, warred with the thrilling sensation of shared freedom, understanding that this new emotional landscape demanded a different kind of leadership. He knew this moment required a more profound, nuanced navigation than his usual confident assertions.

Across the expansive bed, or perhaps just a breath away in the intimate confines of the room, Mark lay still, a stoic sentinel of unspoken longing and simmering conflict. The raw intensity of the night had both fulfilled a secret yearning and deepened the chasm of his unwavering loyalty to Jake, his closest friend. Every shared glance, every fleeting touch, felt like a brand on his very soul, a searing testament to the forbidden fruit now tasted, leaving a bittersweet aftertaste of exhilarating triumph and profound, gnawing guilt. He silently pondered if this audacious new reality would ultimately shatter or irrevocably redefine the very essence of their long-standing brotherhood.

David, ever the pragmatist and keen observer, stretched languidly, a wry, knowing smile playing subtly on his lips. Last night had been an intoxicating symphony of raw, uninhibited desire, a potent and deeply satisfying antidote to his own lingering marital frustrations, a temporary yet profoundly effective escape from the pervasive mundane. He acutely observed the subtle shifts in the room's charged atmosphere, the weighty, pregnant silence, recognizing the delicate dance of complex emotions now unfolding before him. It was a fascinating and visceral study of human desire and its intricate, often complicated aftermath.

A sharper shaft of morning light, bolder now, pierced the heavy curtains, illuminating countless dust motes dancing gracefully in the air, a poignant metaphor for the unsettled particles of their newly forged reality. Jake's eyes, heavy with unspoken questions and burgeoning understanding, met Sarah's across the rumpled, intimately shared expanse, an electric current passing silently between them. Their gaze intertwined, a complex tapestry of question and answer woven into a single, lingering moment, acknowledging the audacious journey they had collectively embarked upon. The air thrummed with the profound weight of unspoken agreements and newly forged, exhilarating connections.

The motel room itself bore silent, vivid witness to the night's passionate unraveling: discarded clothing lay strewn across chairs in a haphazard fashion, empty glasses sat precariously on the bedside table, and the faint, intoxicating scent of whiskey and perfume mingled inextricably in the stale, yet charged, air. It was a tableau of beautiful, uninhibited chaos, a physical manifestation of boundaries blurred, inhibitions delightfully shed, and conventional norms joyfully shattered. This 'Oasis' had indeed offered a temporary refuge, but it had also irrevocably altered the very landscape of their intertwined relationships, leaving a trail of exhilarating, undeniable consequences.

As the first stirrings of the outside world beckoned, the profound realization dawned that the 'Forbidden Trail' was not merely a physical path in the wilderness; it was a metaphorical journey they had just irrevocably begun, a thrilling new reality they now had to navigate on the vast, open road. The resonant hum of their Harleys, typically a powerful symbol of unbridled freedom, would now carry the added, exhilarating weight of shared secrets and burgeoning, audacious desires. Each passing mile would become a silent, poignant testament to the previous night's profound redefinitions, echoing with the echoes of their transformed intimacy.

Sarah, with a newfound boldness, reached out, her fingers gently brushing against Jake's arm, a simple, seemingly innocuous gesture now imbued with a thousand new, complex meanings. Her touch was simultaneously a silent question, a subtle yet powerful affirmation, and a daring, unspoken invitation all at once. Jake, responding instinctively, squeezed her hand, his eyes flicking momentarily towards Mark and David, a silent, profound acknowledgment of the intricate, complex web they had collectively woven. It was a tacit understanding that their adventurous road trip had just taken an electrifying, irreversible turn, charting new emotional territories.

The morning after, far from being an ending, was instead a potent, thrilling beginning, a gateway to uncharted emotional territories and unforeseen relational dynamics. As the sun climbed higher, painting the drab motel room in hues of unexpected promise and exhilarating potential, a collective, silent breath was held, a tacit agreement to bravely confront the intoxicating allure of their new, redefined realities. The open road lay ahead, promising far more than just scenic vistas; it offered a crucible for their transformed passions, daring them to discover precisely how far the forbidden ride truly extended into the very core of their intertwined lives.

The morning light, usually a gentle revealer of new days, felt instead like an intrusive spotlight on Sarah. Her skin still hummed with the echoes of the night, a symphony of touch and daring she hadn't fully anticipated, yet had embraced with a surprising fervor. Lying beside Jake, his steady breathing a familiar comfort, she wrestled with a potent cocktail of exhilaration and unease. The woman who had hesitated at the trip's intensity now felt a thrilling, almost dangerous, sense of liberation. She wondered if this newfound courage was a fleeting spark or the true kindling of a fire within her, one that demanded acknowledgment and perhaps, further exploration. The boundaries, once so clearly defined, had blurred into an intoxicating haze, leaving her both breathless and slightly disoriented.

Jake stirred, the soft rustle of sheets amplifying the silence that now felt profoundly different from the easy comfort they usually shared. He glanced at Sarah, her profile serene in the dim light, and a complex knot of pride and apprehension tightened in his chest. His grand plan to reignite their marriage had certainly taken a turn, a wild, exhilarating detour he hadn't fully mapped out. He wanted Sarah to feel desired, to reclaim the spark, but the shared intimacy with Mark and David had undeniably shifted the landscape, creating a thrilling, yet precarious, new terrain he now had to navigate with a steady hand. The competitive undercurrent he'd always sensed in his friendships now hummed with a new, more potent energy, challenging his very definition of loyalty and possession.

Mark, already awake and dressed, stood by the window, his gaze fixed on the highway stretching into the distance, though his mind replayed the night's events with agonizing clarity. The scent of Sarah, a phantom presence on his skin, was a constant reminder of the lines crossed, the desires indulged. His long-held, unspoken feelings for her had erupted, shattering the carefully constructed dam of his loyalty to Jake. A profound sense of guilt mingled with an undeniable, fierce satisfaction, leaving him in a silent battle between friendship and an almost primal longing. The stoic facade he usually maintained felt impossibly thin, threatening to crack under the weight of his conflicted emotions.

David, ever the pragmatist, was already brewing coffee, his easy-going demeanor a stark contrast to the palpable tension in the room. He observed his friends, a subtle smirk playing on his lips, understanding the unspoken currents swirling between them. For him, the night had been a thrilling release, a testament to the uninhibited exploration of desire, a welcome escape from the frustrations of his own sexless marriage. He found Sarah's beauty intoxicating, her willingness to explore captivating, but his intentions remained rooted in the thrill of the moment, less burdened by the emotional complexities now weighing on Jake and Mark. This adventure, he mused, was certainly delivering on its promise of excitement.

The process of packing and preparing to leave felt like a carefully choreographed dance of avoidance and loaded glances. Each rustle of clothing, each clink of a zipper, resonated with unspoken questions and lingering sensations. Sarah caught Mark's eye across the room, a flicker of understanding passing between them, a silent acknowledgment of the shared secret that now bound them. Jake, ever the leader, tried to project an air of normalcy, his voice perhaps a little too loud as he discussed the next leg of their journey. The air thrummed with a nervous energy, a collective anticipation of how these newly forged dynamics would play out under the harsh light of day and the open road.

Mounting their Harleys felt like a ritual, a return to the familiar, yet everything had fundamentally changed. The roar of the engines, usually a symbol of unbridled freedom, now seemed to amplify the internal chaos within each rider. Jake led the way, his gaze fixed forward, but his mind raced with possibilities and uncertainties. Sarah, riding behind him, leaned into his back, her touch now imbued with layers of shared experience. The scenic highway, once a simple path to adventure, had transformed into a metaphorical journey into uncharted emotional territory, where every mile brought them closer to confronting the true meaning of their redefined relationships.

Sarah, feeling the wind whip through her hair, found a strange clarity amidst the roar of the bike. The initial unease had begun to recede, replaced by a potent sense of self-discovery. She had confronted her own desires, embraced a daring side she hadn't fully acknowledged, and in doing so, had claimed a new agency within her marriage and within herself. The 'hot wife' persona, once a label, now felt like a mantle of power she was learning to wield, demanding a relationship that was vibrant, passionate, and authentically hers. She was no longer just Jake's wife; she was Sarah 'Vixen' Riley, and the road ahead beckoned with tantalizing possibilities for asserting her newfound self.

The group rode in a tighter formation than before, an unspoken pact to continue the journey, yet the camaraderie was underscored by a new, almost electric tension. The thrill of the forbidden, once a distant fantasy, now vibrated in the very air they breathed, a palpable reality they all had to acknowledge. Every stop, every shared glance, every casual remark carried a double meaning, a subtle test of the new boundaries that had been established. The road trip had ceased to be merely an adventure; it had become an intricate, high-stakes dance of desire, loyalty, and the courage to embrace a redefined intimacy.

Jake, sensing the shift in the group's energy, knew he couldn't simply revert to old patterns. His entrepreneurial spirit, always pushing boundaries in business, now demanded the same innovative approach to his personal life. He had sought excitement, but he also genuinely desired a deeper, more profound connection with Sarah, one that transcended mere physical thrills. He realized the journey was not just about rekindling a spark, but about understanding the complex interplay of their desires, acknowledging the courage it took to explore them, and ultimately, forging a bond that was both adventurous and deeply emotionally intimate, a true partnership in every sense.

As the Harleys devoured the miles, the landscape unfurling before them seemed to mirror the unfolding complexities of their relationships. The 'Forbidden Trail' lay ahead, a literal and metaphorical path into further uncharted territory, promising more challenges and revelations. The morning after had merely set the stage for navigating these new dynamics, leaving each character poised on the precipice of profound change. The open road, with its endless horizons, now held the promise of not just adventure, but also the ultimate test of their loyalties, desires, and the very fabric of their intertwined lives.

The morning light, filtered through the motel room's thin curtains, did little to dispel the lingering weight of the previous night. A quiet hum of unspoken questions hung in the air, a tangible presence more potent than the stale coffee brewing in the corner. Jake 'Maverick' Riley watched Sarah 'Vixen' Riley move, her silhouette against the window a study in casual grace, yet he sensed the tremor beneath her composure. Mark 'Rebel' Johnson sat hunched by the door, his usual stoicism now laced with a palpable tension, while David 'Rider' Chen, ever the observer, casually scrolled through his phone, a faint, knowing smile playing on his lips.

Jake cleared his throat, the sound rough in the silence. He had orchestrated this trip, pushing the boundaries, seeking that elusive spark to reignite their passion. The intensity of 'The Oasis' had delivered, undeniably, but now a new, unforeseen current pulsed between them, a dangerous undercurrent he hadn't fully anticipated. A possessive knot tightened in his gut, a subtle reminder that while he wanted excitement, he also needed control, especially when it came to his stunning wife and the hungry eyes of his closest friends.

Sarah, however, felt a strange blend of liberation and trepidation. The night had awakened something primal within her, a sensual power she hadn't truly acknowledged before. She was no longer just Jake's wife, but 'Vixen,' a woman who understood her own desires and the intoxicating effect she had on others. Yet, the path ahead felt uncharted, fraught with emotional landmines. Could they navigate this new terrain without shattering the bonds that held them, and her marriage, together?

Mark finally broke the silence, his voice gravelly. 'That... that was something else, Maverick.' His gaze, however, was fixed on Sarah, a raw, yearning intensity in his eyes that spoke volumes beyond his words. It wasn't a confession, not outright, but a clear acknowledgment of the forbidden line they had all crossed. Jake caught the look, a familiar jealousy flaring, a potent reminder of Mark's long-standing, unspoken attraction to Sarah, now more overt than ever.

David, ever the pragmatic instigator, looked up from his phone, a glint of amusement in his eyes. 'Tell me about it. Lisa would never in a million years...' He trailed off, a sardonic laugh escaping him. 'It's a different kind of freedom, isn't it? When you finally let go of all the 'shoulds' and 'shouldn'ts.' He looked from Jake to Sarah, then to Mark, a silent challenge in his gaze, urging them to confront the new reality they had collectively forged.

Jake decided to address the elephant in the room, albeit carefully. 'We need to talk about... everything,' he stated, his voice firm, though a tremor of uncertainty lingered beneath. 'This trip was about us, Sarah, about finding that fire again. But...' He gestured vaguely, encompassing the entire dynamic now humming between them. He needed to understand if she had found what she sought, and if that quest had led them somewhere he hadn't intended.

Sarah turned to face him fully, her expression unreadable. 'It was about us, Jake. And it was... exhilarating,' she admitted, her voice softer now, more intimate. 'But it also opened my eyes to things I hadn't realized I wanted, things I hadn't dared to explore.' Her gaze flickered to Mark, then back to Jake, a silent confession of the complex desires that had been stirred, a challenge to his perception of her and their relationship.

Jake felt a jolt. He had wanted to reignite passion, yes, but he hadn't anticipated her discovering a passion that might extend beyond him, or at least, beyond the confines he had subconsciously set. He saw the fire in her eyes, a newfound confidence that both thrilled and unnerved him. This wasn't just about rekindling; it was about redefining, about acknowledging a deeper, more adventurous aspect of Sarah that he was only now truly seeing.

The air crackled with the weight of these confessions. Mark shifted uncomfortably, the unspoken tension between him and Jake thick enough to cut with a knife. David merely watched, a silent, knowing presence, the dynamics of their friendship and their marriages now irrevocably altered. The camaraderie they once shared had taken on a dangerous, thrilling edge, a new kind of loyalty now being forged in the crucible of shared, forbidden experiences.

As they packed their bikes, the roar of the Harleys promised not just a return to the open road, but a journey into a new, uncertain future. The 'Forbidden Trail' had led them to 'The Oasis,' and 'The Oasis' had revealed truths that demanded a full reckoning. The conversations and confessions had only just begun, setting the stage for the difficult, exhilarating choices that lay ahead on their road back to reality, and perhaps, to a redefined intimacy.

The Harleys roared to life under a sky painted with the muted hues of dawn, a stark contrast to the fiery passions that had blazed through the night. As Jake 'Maverick' Riley twisted the throttle, the familiar rumble beneath him felt different, imbued with the echoes of shared secrets and whispered desires. The open road, once a symbol of pure freedom, now stretched before them as a path back to a reality irrevocably altered, the very air thick with unspoken words and lingering sensations. Every mile marker seemed to tick off not just distance, but moments of profound, exhilarating, and perhaps terrifying, connection.

Jake's mind raced, the wind whipping past his helmet doing little to clear the heady fog of the previous evening. He had wanted to reignite the spark with Sarah, to push boundaries, but the inferno they'd stumbled into felt both glorious and dangerous. The image of her, vibrant and uninhibited, intertwined with the knowing glances from Mark and David, played on an endless loop. He questioned if this intoxicating blend of arousal and risk was truly what he sought, or if he had inadvertently opened a Pandora's Box, unleashing desires he could barely comprehend, let alone control.

Riding pillion, Sarah 'Vixen' Riley leaned into Jake's back, her body still humming with a potent mix of exhaustion and exhilaration. Her fingers, usually gripping his waist with comfortable familiarity, now felt a new kind of possessiveness, a claim forged in the crucible of shared intimacy. The 'Forbidden Trail' had awakened a part of her she hadn't known was dormant, a sensuality that demanded to be acknowledged, not just by Jake, but by herself. The road back was a journey of self-discovery as much as a return home, forcing her to confront the woman she was becoming.

Behind them, Mark 'Rebel' Johnson rode in a silent torment, the roar of his engine a paltry cover for the tempest raging within him. Every time Sarah shifted, every subtle movement of her body against Jake's, was a fresh stab to his carefully constructed loyalty. The previous night had been a brutal test, one he wasn't sure he had passed unscathed, his long-suppressed desire for Sarah now a raw, exposed nerve. He grappled with the implications, the gnawing question of whether his friendship with Jake could survive the depths of his own forbidden longing.

David 'Rider' Chen, ever the pragmatist, found himself observing the silent drama unfolding on the highway with a detached, yet intrigued, amusement. He'd reveled in the thrill, the uninhibited freedom of the moment, a welcome escape from the sterile confines of his own marital frustrations. While the emotional fallout clearly weighed on Jake, Sarah, and Mark, David found a certain clarity in the chaos. He wondered if this intoxicating taste of the forbidden would lead to true liberation or simply a more complicated cage for his friends.

The camaraderie that had bound them at the start of the trip felt strained, replaced by an unspoken tension that hummed beneath the engines' thrum. Glances in rearview mirrors were no longer casual, but heavy with meaning, fraught with questions and unarticulated feelings. The scenic highway, once a symbol of shared adventure, now felt like a long, winding corridor, each curve a reminder of the intimate boundaries they had collectively obliterated. The freedom of the open road now seemed to amplify their internal confinements, making the silence almost deafening.

Lingering sensations clung to them, an invisible residue of the night's transgressions. A phantom touch, the ghost of a whispered word, the scent of skin on skin – these echoes resonated with the constant vibration of their bikes, a perpetual reminder of the pleasure and the perilous choices made. The physical journey home was merely a vessel for the far more complex emotional voyage each of them was navigating. Their bodies, accustomed to the thrill, now yearned for something more, something undefined but undeniably potent.

As the familiar skyline of the city began to emerge on the horizon, the transition from the wild abandon of the 'Forbidden Trail' to the structured reality of urban life felt jarring. The anonymity of the highway was giving way to the scrutiny of the everyday world, a world where the rules they had bent, or perhaps broken, would once again demand adherence. The casual ease of their departure was replaced by a palpable apprehension, a collective understanding that they couldn't simply park their Harleys and return to their old lives unchanged.

Jake, despite the gnawing uncertainty, felt a strange sense of resolve hardening within him. The adventure had been a gamble, a desperate bid to reignite passion with Sarah, but it had yielded far more than he'd anticipated. He knew they couldn't ignore the seismic shifts that had occurred, the deep emotional fissures and unexpected bridges that had formed between them all. This wasn't just about rekindling a flame; it was about confronting a wildfire, understanding its destructive potential and its capacity for rebirth.

The road back wasn't merely a physical return; it was a profound journey into the heart of their new, complicated reality. The 'Forbidden Trail' had tested their limits, challenged their loyalties, and exposed their deepest desires, leaving them at a precipice. As the roar of their Harleys softened to the familiar hum of city traffic, they understood that the true adventure had only just begun – a perilous path that would either lead to a stronger, redefined intimacy or shatter the very foundations of their relationships.

The hum of the Harleys on the long stretch home felt different, each thrumming engine a reverberation of the night at The Oasis. Jake 'Maverick' Riley gripped his handlebars, the wind whipping past, but his thoughts were less on the open road and more on the uncharted territory he and Sarah had just navigated. He'd craved a spark, an inferno even, to reignite their passion, and the 'Forbidden Trail' had certainly delivered a blaze, scorching old boundaries and forging new, exhilarating ones. The memory of Sarah, vibrant and uninhibited, dancing on the edge of wildness, still sent a primal rumble through him, a satisfaction deeper than he'd anticipated yet laced with a thrilling uncertainty.

Sarah 'Vixen' Riley rode beside him, her helmet shielding a smile that felt both triumphant and a little dangerous. The trip, initially Jake's design, had become her own journey of self-discovery, a potent awakening of desires she'd long kept tethered. She'd always been aware of her allure, but to wield it, to explore its depths with Jake and in the charged presence of their friends, had been liberating. The motel room adventure hadn't just rekindled their connection; it had redefined her understanding of intimacy, pushing her to acknowledge a primal, unapologetic sensuality that now pulsed beneath her skin.

Behind them, Mark 'Rebel' Johnson rode in a familiar silence, yet his stillness was now fraught with a new, complex weight. The unspoken desire for Sarah, a ghost he'd meticulously kept confined, had been given flesh and breath in the intoxicating atmosphere of the trip. He'd witnessed her vibrancy, felt the pull of her magnetic presence, and the raw honesty of the night at The Oasis had both tortured and liberated him. His loyalty to Jake, a bedrock of his life, now felt like a shifting landscape, tested by a truth too potent to ignore, demanding a reckoning he wasn't sure he was ready to face.

David 'Rider' Chen, ever the pragmatic observer, found himself surprisingly contemplative. His usual flirtatious banter felt muted, replaced by a thoughtful assessment of the intense emotional landscape they'd traversed. The raw vulnerability and unbridled passion he'd witnessed, particularly between Jake and Sarah, held a mirror to his own marital frustrations, a stark reminder of the sexual drought with Lisa. He'd been a catalyst, pushing boundaries with playful provocations, but the depth of the others' experiences had opened his eyes to a different kind of thrill, one rooted in genuine, albeit complicated, human connection.

The miles blurred, but the unspoken conversations lingered, weaving through the wind and the engine's roar. Each glance exchanged between Jake and Sarah was a silent dialogue, a negotiation of what had transpired and what it meant for their future. The air between the four of them, once thick with anticipation, was now charged with the residual electricity of shared secrets and altered perceptions. The camaraderie was still there, a strong current, but beneath it flowed a new, powerful undercurrent of redefined loyalties and burgeoning desires that demanded acknowledgment.

Later that evening, back in the quiet sanctuary of their home, Jake found Sarah tracing the lines of his hand, a gesture both familiar and imbued with new meaning. 'So, Maverick,' she murmured, her voice a low purr, 'was that the recommitment you were looking for, or something entirely different?' He pulled her closer, the scent of leather and road still clinging to them, a potent reminder of their journey. He realized his quest for rekindled passion had unearthed something far more profound than just excitement; it had revealed a deeper, more adventurous facet of their bond, a willingness to explore beyond the conventional.

Sarah met his gaze, her eyes sparkling with an unshakeable confidence. 'Because for me,' she continued, 'it felt like a redefinition.

Not just of us, but of me. I found a part of myself out there, a Vixen who isn't afraid to embrace what she truly desires.' Her words were an assertion, a quiet declaration of agency that thrilled Jake to his core. He understood then that this wasn't about him pulling her along; it was about them stepping into a new, shared adventure, both on the road and within the uncharted territories of their intimacy, with her leading as much as he did.

The implications extended beyond their immediate connection, touching the very fabric of their friendships. Mark's quiet intensity, David's knowing glances these were now woven into the tapestry of their lives, undeniable threads that had been pulled and re-tied. The easy, comfortable dynamic of their group had been irrevocably altered, replaced by a more complex, honest understanding of each other's depths and vulnerabilities. They had ventured into the forbidden, and in doing so, had discovered new truths about themselves and their relationships, truths that could not be unlearned.

As the days turned, the memory of the 'Forbidden Trail' and The Oasis didn't fade; it solidified, becoming a cornerstone of their new reality. Jake and Sarah understood that their marriage was no longer confined by unspoken expectations, but had expanded through shared exploration —a commitment to continually seek the edge of their desires together. The question of recommitment had evolved into a bold redefinition, a courageous embrace of an intimacy that was both passionate and profoundly authentic, willing to challenge any boundary that stifled their adventurous spirits.

The open road still called, promising endless horizons and new adventures, but now it held a different resonance for them all. The 'Harley Heartbeats' had indeed found a new rhythm, one that pulsed with the thrill of the forbidden, the courage of redefinition, and the enduring power of a passion rediscovered. The journey ahead was uncertain, but one thing was clear: the path they had chosen was exhilarating, a testament to the fact that true intimacy often began where the conventional ended, and where the heart dared to ride wild.

About the Author

Jake 'Maverick' Riley, a charismatic entrepreneur with a penchant for risk, believes the open road is the ultimate aphrodisiac. Seeking to inject a much-needed spark back into his marriage with the stunning Sarah 'Vixen' Riley, he orchestrates a weekend motorcycle adventure. Joining them are their close friends, the brooding Mark 'Rebel' Johnson, harboring a secret desire for Sarah, and the flirtatious David 'Rider' Chen, looking to escape his own marital frustrations. As their Harleys roar down scenic highways and delve into the 'Forbidden Trail,' the close quarters and intoxicating freedom ignite a dangerous dance of temptation. Jake pushes the boundaries, hoping to rediscover passion with Sarah, but finds himself navigating Mark's simmering jealousy and David's playful provocations. Sarah, initially hesitant, begins to embrace her own desires, finding herself drawn into the charged atmosphere. The bonds of friendship and marriage are tested as unspoken attractions surface, culminating in a night at 'The Oasis' Motel, where loyalties will be challenged and the true meaning of intimacy redefined. This is a spicy, erotic journey into the heart of desire, where the thrill of the forbidden meets the courage to rediscover passion on the ultimate road trip.